George Wolfe Shinn

Stories for the Happy Days of Christmas Time

George Wolfe Shinn

Stories for the Happy Days of Christmas Time

ISBN/EAN: 9783743417502

Manufactured in Europe, USA, Canada, Australia, Japa

Cover: Foto ©Andreas Hilbeck / pixelio.de

Manufactured and distributed by brebook publishing software (www.brebook.com)

George Wolfe Shinn

Stories for the Happy Days of Christmas Time

PREFACE.

The writer of these stories had been in the habit of making *addresses* to young people upon Christmas themes. At length it occurred to him that he could convey the same instruction to them in a much more agreeable way by means of *stories*, and so for some years past the Christmas story has been one of the features of the Christmastide celebrations in our parish. Some of the young people have added to the interest of the stories by illustrating them with tableaux and carols as they have been read aloud at Christmas-tree and other entertainments.

And now the stories are printed in the hope that they may add to the Christmas joy of other homes, and especially of other gatherings of young folks at Christmas-tide.

NEWTON, MASS.,
Christmas, 1879.

CONTENTS.

to try. But perhaps if you were to get a look at him you would have a better idea of his appearance than my description can give you. [1. See page 207.]

Now this odd creature had a sister who was equally odd.

She was a thin, pinched old body; with very white hair, and a very pale face.

Her dress was after a style of her own. I could not begin to describe it, only I know its waist was up under her arms and its skirt was very scanty. She had a cap with a great broad frill to it, and wore glasses of the same sort as her brother's, and always carried an umbrella when she went out. But really I can not describe her to you so as to give you any idea how she looked. You should have seen Aunt Susan for yourselves, as her brother and she took a walk together as they used to do, some of the pleasant days at sunset. [2.]

Now this odd couple lived in a house that was just as quaint as they were. It was long and low and rambling. It had more than seven gables, nine chimneys, plenty of porches, bird boxes on every peak and under the eaves, and five front doors painted yellow.

It was not built all at once, but it grew by degrees, just as Uncle John took a fancy to add something to it. No architect would plan a house like it. Perhaps no one would employ an architect to do so, although after all it was a comfortable old place. It stood on a hill and was surrounded by great tall poplar-trees that looked like a line of sentinels keeping guard over the place.

Uncle John's lands were quite extensive. There was a broad meadow, and great fields for grass and grain, and off to the north side a strip of woods.

All around the house were the flower gardens, where the most amazing hollyhocks, sunflowers, and marigolds bloomed, and great beds of all sorts of fragrant herbs,—thyme, and sweet-marjorum, and sage. Aunt Susan and Uncle John spent a great deal of time in this garden in pleasant weather, and they evidently considered it a marvel of beauty.

One of the most notable things about Uncle John was the wonderful care he took of dumb animals, poor castaways and outcasts that no one else would have about.

His barns and grounds were a sort of nursery for crippled dogs and old horses. Whenever he came across some poor, miserable brute that had a broken leg, or that was injured in any way, he would give it shelter until it got well. Cats that had no home found a refuge in his barns. Old horses that unfeeling owners had turned out on the roadside to die were sure of a good stall and plenty of feed if Uncle John only saw them. The only bother to him was that he could not get rid of these creatures when they got better.

There were as many as a dozen dogs around at one time. The cats no one tried to count, and the horses nearly filled up all the stalls of the barn. Now and then he would get rid of a horse by presenting some poor farmer with one he had doctored up until it was strong enough to do a little work, but he never gave any of these poor creatures away without first exacting a written pledge that its new owner would treat it well.

His sympathy, however, did not confine itself to dumb animals, but his hired help for his farm and his house servants were almost all people whom no one else could get along with. They were deaf, or lame, or had some infirmity of mind or of body that made it hard for them to live with any one, except Uncle John and Aunt Susan. These two good old people managed to bear with their infirmities and made them happy.

I want to describe some of the queer people Uncle John picked up, and employed as helpers. His cook had once been noted throughout all the neighborhood for her bad temper. She could howl like a wildcat, and every body feared her. Uncle John once heard her in one of her stormiest moods, and was not contented until he had transferred her to his own kitchen. She was just the person he wanted there. and by and by she became usually as gentle as a lamb. It was odd though to see her mixture of lamblike gentleness and tiger ferocity. [3.]

There was old Dickey Diggs, the most stupid old creature that ever wore a hat. He wasn't an idiot. He was only stupid, blundering, forgetful, twisted, absent-minded. He would sometimes lead the wheelbarrow out to the pump to give it a drink, thinking it was a horse. Once he was seen harnessing himself up in the cart while the sober donkey stood looking on amazed. One day Uncle John sent him to grease the cart wheels, but by some twist or other Dickey forgot what he was sent to do, and placed the grease in the oven, thinking perhaps it was a pudding. [4.]

The two other servants I will describe were twin sisters whom Uncle John discovered in one of his visits to a distant city. They were unlike in every particular. One

was tall, the other was short. The motions
of the tall one were as quick as the wind,
those of the little one were as slow as a
snail.

Uncle John took a fancy to them because
neither of them would be separated from the
other, and no one wanted the two as servants, especially as they found it hard to
learn any thing. One could not do any
thing without the help of the other sister.
Although so unlike, there was a singular de-
pendence of one upon the other which made
them inseparable. [5.]

Now think what a strange household it
was when they were all together. [6.]

When Uncle John went off his own prem-
ises, he usually rode on horseback. Where he
went, or why he went, no one knew. Some
of the folks said that he only went out to
see if he could find any old horse adrift, or
to intercept any boys who were on their way
to the pond to drown a kitten. It was very

true that he frequently came back bringing some trophy, some poor creature, human or brute, to be nursed and cared for.

Every body knew him, and every body laughed as his odd form, mounted on a great awkward horse, came in sight. He was not a very graceful rider, and his favorite horse wasn't a bit graceful. Every one wondered why he did not ride a better beast, one with a gentler gait, that would not bump him up and down as this awkward creature did. But he rather enjoyed it, and so for years the people became accustomed to seeing him perched up on the tall rump of the ugly beast. But they would smile at the ridiculous figure he cut if they saw him twenty times a day. No one could become indifferent to the funny sight. Strangers and residents would turn to look and then would enjoy a laugh at the odd spectacle. Odd enough it was, for the horse beside being very tall was very long, and his gait was utterly indescribable. It was something between a trot and a roll. He got over the ground fast enough, unless

he took a notion to stop and graze along
the roadside when he espied some especially sweet-looking grass. On these occasions, and they were pretty frequent, Uncle
John would patiently wait until the beast
was ready to go on again. Every stream
they crossed, the horse must stop for a drink,
and he took such an enormous quantity
of water you would have thought he must
surely burst.

Now Uncle John, with all of his queer
fancies and odd surroundings, was the richest man in the county. None of his wealth
had come to him by inheritance. He had
earned it all by his own hard work, and
Aunt Susan, his sister, had saved it carefully
for him.

He had not lived very long in the village of Elms when I became acquainted
with him. He had come there from a distant city, a retired tea merchant, to spend
the rest of his days, according to his own
tastes, or in carrying out some notions of
his own.

The people soon learned to like the dear old man and his sister, and though their appearance always made mirth, no one ever was rude to them. The beggars found out his generous spirit, and not one of them ever went hungry from his doors. There were no "tramps" in those days.

Well, Uncle John soon became the good friend of every body for miles around, and not a man or boy but would return pleasantly the hearty salutation which he had for them all when he met them.

Week by week he and his sister would be seen going to the little chapel in the village, and none were more devout in their worship, or more respectful hearers than they. It is true their solemn march up the side aisle in their queer garments would always make people smile, but then no one would have given them offence for a great deal. It is also true that Uncle John's voice did not improve the singing any for he would always sing in such sepulchral bass tones that they seemed to come up from the cellar.

However, every body said he was a good
man, and they would not worry him by check-
ing his attempts to be musical.

Well, one Christmas time about five years
after Uncle John and Aunt Susan came to
live in our village, every one of the villagers
was surprised to receive an invitation to a
Christmas party which was to be given by
Uncle John at his house, on the next night
after Christmas. There was a great stir, and
of course much wondering as to what would
be done, and how they would enjoy themselves, and how it would all end. But nearly every one concluded to go anyhow; and, as
it grew dark on the day after Christmas, people were seen going in all directions towards
Uncle John's house. The wonder is how the
house could hold so many, but it was a great
rambling building, and he had had carpenters at work for months past at some mysterious extensions of which no one could
guess the use. It was very unlike an ordinary house, for as they passed to the

upper floor to lay aside their hats and wrappings they saw great long rooms with rows of little beds, and right in the middle was one room fitted up with benches, for all the world like a chapel.

Uncle John received his guests in the great parlor down-stairs, and made them feel at home at once by his lively, jolly, whole-souled welcome. Great fires were blazing on the hearths, and beneath the influence of the host and the genial warmth of the fires all began to feel very comfortable, but now and then a strange hush was evident, as if all expected some odd *denouement* of this unusual party. But as games and music were introduced, and supper was served, they began to conclude it was *only a party* and that Uncle John was trying to be neighborly in his way. Towards nine o'clock, however, there was a bustle caused by the arrival of two strangers, both wrapped in great overcoats and shawls as if they had ridden far that cold night.

Uncle John met them at the door and drew

them in. That one must be a lawyer some
one whispered. See the green bag he car-
ries. Yes, he was a lawyer, but such a queer
looking lawyer. Where did Uncle John find
him ? [7.]

The other one of these strangers certainly
must be a doctor.

Here he comes with his box of surgical
instruments and his phials of medicines. [8.]

Uncle John led the two strangers off to
give them some refreshments, and the village people went on with their games and
plays and talk, though much wondering why
these strangers had come and who they were.

In the course of half an hour or so, Dickey
Diggs appeared, evidently charged with some
message to the guests, but he had forgotten
it, and had to go back to see what he had
been sent to say. When he came back, it
was with the request that Uncle John wanted every body to go down-stairs; but while
they wondered at this strange request, Uncle

John himself appeared, and told them they
were to come up-stairs, and not to go to the
cellar. Of course there was a laugh at poor
Dickey's blunder, but they all mounted the
stairs sure now that the interest of the evening was approaching its highest point whatever it might be, but no one could guess
what it was.

They found the rooms up-stairs brilliantly
lighted, and as many as could be seated were
asked to occupy the benches in the middle
room, while the others sat on chairs and on
the little beds in the rooms to the right and
the left which opened into the main room by
folding doors.

Occupying chairs at the upper end of the
main room were Uncle John and the two
strangers.

Now if you will imagine that we are the
villagers seated in these queer upper rooms
of the old building, we will try to look at the
group in the upper end of the main room as
it appeared when all things were ready. [9.]

When all had become quiet, Uncle John arose, and this is what he said:—

"My friends, I know I am an odd old fellow, and have odd ways of doing things; but if I can't do things in my own way, I am like all the rest of the world,—I think they are not well done. You are all wondering why this house is fixed up as it is, and what is to be done with it. Before I tell you that, I must tell you a story.

"Many a long year ago, when Susan· and I were children, we had a little sister. We three were poor neglected orphans, turned out into the world at the death of our parents to seek our own living.

"The only thing we had as we thus went out, beside the scanty clothing we wore, was a poor old crippled dog. He clung to us. He had been our pet, and we could not turn him away. Neither would he desert us, but in all of our wanderings he was with us.

"I will not describe all the sad experiences of the months and months of our poverty,—

how we sought work and failed to find it, how we begged from door to door, until at length, to make our sorrows still worse, my little sister was run over in the street by a heavy team, and was an invalid for the rest of her life. But her misfortuné brought us friends. I found a place in a store and Susan in a good family, and little Margery was carried to a hospital.

"By and by we found lodgings with a respectable family, and my wages grew gradually better, until we could furnish a room or two.

"Day by day was my toil lightened by the thought of spending the long evenings at home with my sisters. Margery was just able to make her way about the room upon her crutches, but her sunny smile never failed her. The sunshine of heaven seemed ever to rest upon her, and she seemed to me to have the halo around her head before she reached the land of brightness. Our old dog was with us, and had his place by the fireside. He was my sister's friend and pet. Although

old and crippled, we could not turn him off,
nor did we wish to do so.

"Ah, how well do I remember those years,
—as steadily rising in business I was able to
add to our invalid sister's comfort, and smooth
her decline. But she faded away before our
eyes, and the night after our most happy
Christmas Day we found her dead in her
chair, and the old dog at her feet. She had
gone quietly to her rest, and her dumb companion had ceased to live when he found his
mistress was gone."

Here the old man paused in his story, and
the sobs of his hearers prevented his going
on for some minutes, but he presently re-
sumed, and said—

"This was years ago, and I was a young
man then. Now I am old, and have not
many years to live ere I shall join her in a
better land. Her memory has ever been with
me, and I have seen her face in every sufferer I have met. Yes, you have often wondered at my strange fancy for poor dumb
animals, but I have ever remembered her

love for the old dog Jack who was our friend in our poverty.

"And now that wealth has been given me, I am going to devote it to the service of the dear Christ in befriending his little ones. This building in which you are now met is to be a Children's Hospital. Here is the chapel where they will be taught to love the Saviour, there are the beds where they will sleep. The rooms down-stairs where you first assembled are for the other purposes of the little folks when well enough to be about and to play. And here is the doctor who is to take charge of the hospital, and, if God will, make them well."

At this point the doctor seated by Uncle John arose and bowed to the audience. Then when he was seated the old gentleman went on—

"And now I have asked my lawyer to come here to-night to read the deed of gift, and the plan of this charity which in your presence to-night is thus formally opened.'

Here the other gentleman arose, and, open-

ing the bag which he carried, read out a
long and dry legal document, in which it
was recited that John Marcon of such a
place and of such a county, for the purpose
of founding a hospital for children to be
known as "The Margery Marcon Hospital"
did give to such and such a board of trus-
tees, the house and grounds in such a place,
and beside, the sum of a great many thou-
sands of dollars, to be by them and their
successors held in trust, &c.

It was a very formal document, and almost formidable from the number of its legal
terms, but its drift was comprehended after
the lawyer had made a few explanations, and
then what a shout arose from young and
old! Why it was fortunate that there were
no sick children there yet. And then, when
the noise had subsided, there was such a
rush to shake Uncle John's hand! The happiness of that moment would have repaid
him for the good deed, but he had with him
the thought that somehow the soul of the
departed sister was rejoicing in Paradise

over what he had done. Certain it was that the good Christ saw it, and that was reward enough.

And now many years have passed since that Christmas time, and the little white beds are full of children who have been brought to the Margery Marcon Hospital to be made well; but in two white beds,— yes, under the snow,—the bodies of Uncle John and Aunt Susan are sleeping the sleep from which they will never awaken till they hear the trumpet of the archangel at the last great day.

THE TRAMPS' CHRISTMAS EVE

THE TRAMPS' CHRISTMAS EVE.

NEARLY a year before the Christmas Eve of which I am to tell you, the home of Farmer Warren was made very sad by the departure of his son William. Perhaps the boy was very foolish to go away as he did, but the disappointment he felt at being rejected by the girl whom he had loved ever since she came as a little stranger to his father's house, was so bitter that he hastily tore himself away from his old home, and from the day he left only one message had been received from him, and that was a brief letter stating that he was trying to forget his sorrow by working in the silver mines of Nevada. He was

very foolish for going away, for the orphan.
Mary Louise, had refused him only because
she was afraid his parents would object to
his marrying one who came to them a poor
parentless child from the almshouse of a
great city.

She did not know then how she had grown
into their hearts, and that they had long
regarded her as their daughter, and would be
glad indeed to see her become their son's
wife.

But she, poor little soul, thought only of
herself as an orphan of whose parentage no
one knew any thing, not even the keepers of
the almshouse where she had been left one
winter's night by some stranger. All the
information given about her was a note written in a scrawling hand containing these
words: "This here baby ain't got no father
and no mother. Both of 'em is ded."

The keeper of the almshouse took the baby
in, and she was christened Mary Louise, after
the name of his wife, and as no one knew
her family name, the Mary stood for the

Christian name, and Louise had to serve for the family name.

She stayed at the almshouse until she was eight years old, when Farmer Warren, thinking his wife ought to have some one to wait on her a little, drove up one day, was pleased with the sweet, innocent face of the little girl, and took her to his home. There she grew up and ripened into a beautiful young woman, graceful, active, and intelligent. She had made good use of all her advantages, and, although her position was nominally that of a servant in the family, she was treated as a daughter, and well repaid the affection of the old couple whose wants she so carefully looked after. As time went on, she grew to be the main-stay of the house. Her busy brain and active fingers gave shape to all the details of the great farmhouse, and her cheery voice directed the labor of the servants that were employed.

It was amazing how one so young could do so much, and the old farmer used to declare that her muscles were made of steel, and her brain was equal to managing a colony.

How bright and happy she made that old farmhouse, and how the old folks leaned upon her for support as they felt themselves tottering down the other side of the hill of time!

All this pleasant state of things might have gone on no one knows how much longer if she had not refused to become William Warren's wife. And she never would have refused him if she had not been afraid of bringing disgrace upon him by letting him marry one who did not know even the name of her parents, and who had spent seven years of her life in an almshouse. There is where she made her mistake, for no one cared who her parents were, nor where she had spent her baby days. It was enough for them all to know that she was now a noble woman.

But she said "no" to William, and he took it as her final answer, and left his home.

How changed that home became after he

went away! The brightness died out of his father's face, and the poor old mother grew more feeble day by day. ·The farm work did not go on well without him, and he was terribly missed every hour.

Old Mr. Warren tried every plan to hear something more from his son. He wrote in all directions to the mines of the Pacific, but no word came, and now it was nearly a year since William went away. Yes, nearly a whole sad year, for he had gone the day following the last Christmas, and it was now almost Christmas again.

We look in upon them as the three sat in the living room of the old farmhouse two nights before Christmas. [1.]

The old people are at opposite sides of the fireplace where the logs are burning, both wrapped in their own gloomy thoughts, and Mary is seated at a table, busy with some sewing, but now and then the great tears blind her eyes and the work falls down into her lap.

The silence which has lasted long is broken by the old man, who says:

"Mary, what shall we do about this here merry-making that they want to have in our kitchen to-morrow night? You know to-morrow is Christmas Eve, and Betty says they want to keep up the old ways of havin some of the folks come in just as they used to do."

"Oh, Mr. Warren," she replies, "why do you ask me! I feel as if I could never be merry again. I don't know what to say. I'll do any thing you think is right, but I've no heart for mirth."

"Well, well, poor girl, I know ye is sad; but you're the manager since mother and I is gettin' old, and I consult ye about every thin'. I don't know how to refuse the folks what they've asked, but I'd rather they wouldn't have it. Howsomever, I s'pose it ain't right for us to deprive 'em of the chance of havin' a pleasant evenin', but I wish— Oh! I wish my boy was here!"

And here the old man broke down and

wept, and the good wife moaned in sympathy.

For a long time after no words were spoken, all were busy with their own thoughts, but there came a knock at the door and roused them. Presently there entered a deputation to ask the accustomed privilege of a Christmas jollification in the kitchen. [2.]

Nothing could exceed the awkwardness of the three who stood grinning and bowing, and mustering up courage to present the petition which had been drawn up on a paper.

It was a written petition which Jonas Green, the man of all work, who was something of a poet, or who thought he was, had spent the whole evening in writing.

Like many another, Jonas was immensely pleased with his own productions, but having a high voice and defective eyesight, he was not a very impressive reader, but he thought he was. With him came Betty,—mischievous, fun-loving Betty,—who had flattered the poet, and made him think his verses ranked

with those of the poets in the old school-
book which Jonas thumbed so industriously.

Poor Jonas drank in with great greedi-
ness the flattery—and as one had described
the poet as rolling his eyes in fine frenzy,
so Jonas tried to roll his, but they were too
weak to roll much, and when he did roll
them, the effect back of the queer pair of
spectacles he wore was ludicrous enough.

The other member of the kitchen com-
mittee was Michael. Good, honest, blundering old Michael, from the sod of Erin, a genuine Irishman, warm-hearted and faithful.

You could not mistake him for any one
else than a Hibernian, so broad was the
brogue, and so marked was his appearance.
And now these three stood before Mr. Warren to secure his consent to having the usual
frolic in the kitchen on Christmas Eve.

"Well, Jonas, what now?" asked Mr.
Warren, and then the poet unfolded the
paper in his hand, and began to read.

"Illustrious and wennerrable farmer,
  The day arter to-morrer
    Is called Christmas Day.
Now Christmas comes but once a year,
And we most humbly do appear
    To ax you if we may
On Christmas Eve together in
Your great big, great big, kitchyin
    Our friends invite
To spend a socyal hour or two
In doin' as we've youst for to do
    On that air night.
A little corn we'll pop
And then perhaps we'll stop
    And tayles and stories tell,
With games and plays and songs
The moments roll along
    And all end well."

The manner in which Jonas delivered
these lines was so irresistibly comic that
the hearts that had been so sad before now
grew merry, and impulsively the old farmer
spoke up and said, " Yes, yes, my man, have
just as good a time as you can, and joy be
with you always."

Then Jonas and Betty and Michael, the deputation, withdrew, but they had for the time driven away all sad thoughts from the minds of the three by the fireside, and the talk that lasted till bedtime was more cheerful than it had been, until at length the old mother said, " I did not say any thing while you and Mary was talkin', but somehow I've had a feelin' comin' over me that things will be better for us than they has bin. Suthin' tells me that William won't allers stay away from us. He knows we two is gettin' old, and I expect to see him ag'in afore I die." Her hopeful words gave hope to the other two, and they went to their rest feeling as they had not felt in a long time before, and from three hearts there went up very fervent prayer for the absent one.

What an uproarious time they had in that old kitchen on Christmas Eve! There were Jonas and Betty and Michael, and five of their friends, and they made the old kitchen ring with their laughter as they sat around the fire popping corn and telling stories. [3.]

How easy it is for people upon a winter's
night, as the wind goes howling by, to drift
into telling ghost stories; and so these folks
before they knew it were fairly absorbed in
the details of one of Michael's most frightful
yarns. Michael was a famous story teller.
In fact, he was so fond of relating his weird
Irish tales that he would lean on his plough
handle, or stop his team at any time, to cur-
dle up some one's blood with one of his
strange yarns that he had heard in the old
country.

Now as he told his story this Christmas
Eve, the circle drew their chairs closer and
closer together as if to protect each other,
should one of Michael's wonderful ghosts
glide in upon them. It was a strange yarn
that he was spinning, full of contradictions
and absurdities. It ran somehow thus:

"Ghosts, is it ye is talkin' about? Sure
an' it's in the ould counthree that there is
many a ghost. In the ould castles and inns
there is many of 'em.

"I've never been after seein' any of 'em

myself, but I've seen people that has heard
'em.

"Now there's Bridget Marooney, my own
sister's husband's cousin, she that married
Bryan O'Rourke, sure now Bridget has been
tellin' me many's the time that the ould inn
with the sign of the stag's head had a ghost
in its best room where the ould furniture
was that onst belonged to the castle. Nobody ever seed the ghost that used to come
there, but many's the thraveller that's been
wakened up in the middle of the night by a
bangin' at the windy and an awful groanin'.

"It's thrue enough that one thraveller got
up when he heard the bangin' and said it
was nothin' but the limb of the ould tree
that would strike the windy shutter when
the wind blowed. But shure no one be-
lieved him; for if an ould room in an ould
inn with ould furniture that's been in a
castle ain't the place for a ghost, where
would yes expect a ghost to be? It's ould
inns that ghosts loves to live in, and Bridget
Marooney often heard the bangin' and the

groanin' when she went into that room to swape it up; and Bridget Marooney is a girrel that tells the truth, barrin' the times that she takes a dhrop of the crayter from the flask of whiskey that some thraveller has forgotten to take away with him in the mornin'.

"'Bridget,' says I, 'now tell me sure an', what did ye hear in the ould room?' An' she says, says she, 'I heard the bangin' at the windy, and an awful groanin' as if somebody was bein' killed.' 'And where was the groanin'?' says I. 'Why,' she says, says she, 'it seemed to be in the ould chimbly.'

"But the thraveller that said the bangin' was made by the wind blowin' the limbs of the tree ag'in the windy said that the groanin' was made by the wind down the chimbly,—but how can the wind groan? The wind ain't got feelin' like a human bein'. The wind don't get hurted and cry out.

"You see, Bridget is a wonderful woman, if I do say so that thinks of goin' back to

Ireland and marryin' her if she will make up her mind to give up touchin' the whiskey. But I'm afeard she likes a dhrop of the cray-ter too well to give it up, and she has a way of throwin' things around when she gets mad that used to make me afeard of her. But for all o' that she's a wonderful woman, and she can argy with the praist, and nobody can make her believe that a limb of a tree can bang like that ag'in a windy, and that the wind can groan down a chimbly like a human bein'.

"An' all the neighbors says the raysan that room is haunted is because the ould miser that used to live in it was a thafe, and some bigger thafe stold his money and he died from the loss of it. And now he comes back ag'in, a-lookin' fur it, and beatin' his head ag'in the walls of the house, and groan-in' because he can't find it where he used to count it all out, the bright pieces of gould and siller, in the big chist by the side of his bed. The mane heretic, Dennis M'Dade, used for to say that he didn't know what the ould miser's ghost wanted with his money anyhow. But what did such a heretic as Dennis know about the wants of a ghost?

"Sure an' he might be seekin' for it to distribute it among the desarvin' females sech as Bridget, that they could make good use of it to build a mansion and buy a patch of praity land, and marry sech as me that would make 'em good husbands.

"For sure if Bridget had the ould man's money, I could forgive her the offence of throwin' things around when she had been drinkin' too much of the crayter.

"Sure an' then I'd be one of the gintry, an would ride around in me coach with a futman standin' up at the back of me lady and me."

How accurately then Michael went on to describe the experiences of certain travellers who had been kept awake all night long by this fearful whack, whack, whack, against the window! And to give greater effect to his story just then Michael said,

"It was a noise jest like this now," and

he pounded against the side of the kitchen table.

Just as he had finished, there came three rousing whacks at the kitchen door. Terror seized upon all the party, for they thought at once that a ghost had come, so full had their minds been of Michael's story, and they started up all trembling. Their hair seemed to stand on end, their knees shook together. They looked at each other in blank astonishment, and then the three great raps came again, and a voice outside called, "Open your door. Let us in, can't you?" The voice was not ghostlike, but heavy and gruff. It drove away their thoughts of ghosts, and made them see how foolish they were to be so frightened.

For awhile, however, no one would open the door, but finally Jonas drew the bolt, and in stepped two of the most tattered, dilapidated individuals you ever saw. [4.]

They were all in rags, and their faces were covered with a great growth of beard. No sooner had they stepped in than Betty whis-

pered, "they're tramps. We'll all be killed."
And at once the company was filled with
greater terror than before, for a living tramp
had grown to be an object of more fear than
a dead ghost.

What a commotion there was in the kitch-
en: the women screaming, the men springing for any article that would serve as a
weapon in case the tramps proved troublesome; but they did not look as if they would
be troublesome at all, for there they stood
laughing and enjoying the commotion they
had created.

It would be hard to describe the appearance of these two men. They were the most
disreputable looking of all the tramp species.
Each had a bundle over his shoulder on a
stick, and they wore hats that had evidently
gone on from bad to worse until they could
not be any worse.

Well, there these two strangers stood, enjoying the terror of the others, until at
length Betty, who seemed to be more cour-
ageous than the rest, spoke up, " Well, now

4

that you've gin us a good skeer—what do ye want?"

"Shelter from the cold," replied one; "we've travelled far to-day and are tired and cold. Let us sit down by your fire. We're harmless fellows. We don't want to hurt any one. It's an awful night outside, and it seems warm and pleasant here. Will you let us stay awhile?"

Permission was very unwillingly granted, but it seemed too cruel to turn them out into the winter's storm, and so they stayed.

The strangers had an easy way of making themselves at home. They slung their bundles into a corner, put their hats under their chairs, and found the warmest seats by the fire. It was some time, however, before the merry-makers in the kitchen could dismiss their fears of the two strange guests, but by the time these dilapidated travellers had eaten with great relish some slices of gingerbread that Betty had brought out, the dread of them had gone, and the strangers proceeded in their way to make themselves agreeable. This they did by telling stories of their adventures; thrilling stories they were, not quite so startling as Michaels ghost stories, but so fascinating that the company drew closer around them and listened with rapt attention.

One of the stories told that night was—

THE PASSAGE OF THE LONG DARK TUNNEL.

It ran about like this:—

"Yes, I've had many strange adventures in my time, but the one that frightened me most of all was when I tried to pass through the long dark tunnel at night. It was a short cut from the main road to the village, and was shorter by nearly a mile than the usual way.

"I knew it was dangerous, but I was in a hurry, and thought I would try it, so I entered the mouth of the long dark passage, and trudged on. It was dripping with water, and smelled horribly. I stumbled over the cross-ties, and once I fell down flat, but these were small troubles compared with

what was to come; for after I had got about
half way through I heard the screech of the
engine coming in at the other end, and soon
I saw the light like the great mocking eye
of an advancing monster. Well, I can't tell
you how I felt, or how fast the thoughts
went through my brain. It seemed an age
while I stood there watching that rapidly
approaching light, and listening to the thun-
dering of the train as it came on and on. I
had no other expectation than that of being
killed. It seemed impossible to escape an
awful death. I could not hope to squeeze
myself near enough to the walls of the tunnel, and of course I could not stop the train.
For awhile I stood fascinated, unable to stir
hand or foot, but as the train came rattling
on I could not endure the sight of that great
mocking eye, and so I dashed myself down
flat on my face on the ground.

"I held my breath and waited for the awful blow that would end my life, and then I
lost all consciousness. How long I stayed
there flat in the black puddle of water where

I had fallen, I knew not, but when my senses came back to me the train had passed and I was safe. Yes, safe; for, in falling down, I had fallen between the double tracks in a place worn away by a stream that had washed a passage for itself, and so I escaped. A few inches to the right or left, and I would not have been here to-day to tell the tale."

One story led on to another, and each story grew more exciting than the last, but after awhile there was a pause, during which the younger of the two strangers glancing up saw over the kitchen fireplace a violin, and took it down and began to tune it. When they found he could play, they were urgent that he should play them a tune, and he willingly complied; but such a comical figure did he cut as he sawed away with the bow on the old violin, that they laughed until the tears rolled down their cheeks. Presently it was proposed by Betty that they should have a dance, and they arranged themselves for an old Virginia reel.

The fiddler sat perched upon a flour bar-
rel on one side, and the other stranger took
his place in the line for the dance.

And now the fun grew uproarious, for
never were there such jolly dancers as these.
Their bodies swayed back and forth. They
swung their arms, and frisked about as if
they were possessed. It is hard to describe
the mirth that came into that old kitchen, as
the merry dancers went through the figures
of the reel.

In the midst of the uproar, old Farmer
Warren and his wife and Mary, attracted
by the noise, came in to look on at the jollification. [5.]

As they came in, there was a rapid change
in the conduct of the strangers, and the fiddler became embarrassed and lost the tune.
The dance stopped. All eyes were turned
upon the two tramps, who had drawn close
together. There was a pause, a dead silence
for a few minutes, when the old farmer said,
"Go on, my friends, go on; don't stop. Let
me too enjoy your happiness."

But the strangers stood still, side by side, and then, turning to each other, began the strangest sort of performance. The larger of the two started to run for the door, but the other caught him, and then began a scuffle. And, to the surprise of every one, off came the wigs that they had worn.

In an instant there was a scream from Mary. "It's William," she said, and she caught him by the arms.

Sure enough it was William; come home again after the long year's absence,—come home in this strange disguise on Christmas Eve,—come home to stay.

But why such a strange return? Why in disguise at all? Why with such an odd companion?

Motioning to them all to be seated, he told his story, and this is how it ran:—

"You all know why I went away. I felt that I could not stay here another day, and so I resolved that I would try to forget my bitter disappointment among new scenes and with new surroundings. I made my way to the great West, and finally to the mines of Nevada. I cared very little to make money, but wanted to forget my trouble in active employment. I had not been long in the mines before a dreadful accident happened,— the earth caved in and I was saved from death only by the efforts of this my friend, John Wallace.

"From that day there sprang up a strong affection between us, and I told him my story and he told me his. Well, the result was that he persuaded me to come home again, and we made our way by slow degrees, seeing what we could as we came along, and timed our return so as to reach here on Christmas Eve. I can not tell you how deep were my emotions upon nearing my home. So when we got to the village, we concluded to disguise ourselves, and what you see upon us, these rags and tatters, we bought at an old shop, and came here so changed that I knew no one would know me. I wanted to get into the old house once more, and finding the kitchen lighted up, we

entered and have tried to add to the enter-
tainment of Betty and her friends.

"When you, father and mother and Mary,
came in, my courage failed me, and I tried
to run away, but my friend John stopped
me as you know, and kept me here, and
now here I am. The welcome Mary has
given me shows me how foolish I was to
have gone away at first, and your letter
which reached me only two months ago,
just before I concluded to return, explains
why she said that cruel "no." I am sure
she will change her mind,—yes, that she has
changed it, and all will be well,—especially
after she hears another story which John
Wallace is now ready to tell you."

And now all eyes were turned to the other
stranger, the fiddler, and this is what he
said:—

"I'm an old sailor. I've sailed from port
to port these many years. I married Rose
Murray in England, and left her money to
cross the ocean in a steamer to join me

in New York, for there our vessel was to sail.

"I never saw her again, for the vessel in which I sailed was lost at sea, and I was rescued by a brig bound on a whaling voyage of four years in the South Pacific.

"When I came back to New York at the end of the four years, I found that Rose had landed there from the steamer, and had gone to the people where I had engaged a place for her; but after the birth of her little girl she heard of the loss of the vessel in which I had sailed, and thought me dead; her heart was broken and she died.

"So the people where she boarded carried the little one to an almshouse, but no one could tell me where, for Rose's friends had moved far away to the West. At last I found them and learned the place. Then when I went to it to see her, she had been taken away by a farmer, they said—a farmer named Warren, but the record was lost and they knew not where he lived. [6.]

"And so for many years I searched for my

daughter, and had begun to think I could never find her, when I met William in the mines, and found that my daughter was safe in his father's house. I persuaded him to return, and here we are. It was his plan to assume this disguise, for wise as he is upon all other matters, his head was well nigh turned because he was afraid he would not be welcomed by the one who once refused to become his wife.

"Mary, you will not disgrace him, for you are an honest sailor's daughter, and your mother was a jewel.

"And this is my daughter," continued he, "my daughter whom I never saw before to-night, but she is her mother's very image. Her eyes, her hair, her face, just as eighteen years ago I married her in the old home where we were children together.

"Mary, thank God I've found you! Often and often I've been ready to despair, but now I've found you, and the Lord be praised!"

"Aye," said the old farmer, "aye, the

Lord be praised who has brought so much joy to us this Christmas Eve. He has sent me back my boy, and he has helped you in this strange way to find your daughter. And perhaps he has permitted us to have this strange experience of joy to-night that we may all the better on to-morrow's festival know what it means when it is declared that God sent his Son into the world to save the lost and to bring the *wanderers home*."

THE BELATED CHRISTMAS GUESTS.

THE BELATED CHRISTMAS GUESTS.

ANY long years ago when much of
the central and northern part of
the state of New York was an
unbroken wilderness, before the
great forests were cut away, and before rail-
roads made a net-work between the different
sections of the state,—three families removed
from a town near the southern border and
took up their abode in one of the counties
along the Mohawk.

They were pious families, and had many
a regret at leaving the dear old church
where for so many years they had wor-
shipped the God of their fathers. But there
were many young mouths to feed, and the
hope of feeding them led to the formation

of new homes in the newer region where not so many strugglers for bread were to be found, and where the bread might perhaps be the more easily won.

The lands they purchased were in the same county, but the rough houses they built were distant from each other some miles. Roads were few, most of them being winding ways along the river bank, or through the woods. There was but little open country, and few neighbors. Cleared spaces were the exception.

During the summers, there was some little intercourse between the three families, but winter snows were so deep and winter colds so sharp that they saw but little of each other in the cold season, except at Christmas time.

It became their custom always to assemble at the house of one of the three the day before Christmas, and to spend Christmas, and a day or two more, in happy festivities.

There being no church near, they would read the church service in the family room.

talk together of the wondrous birth of the Redeemer, and have many merry games and happy times generally.

Bright days were those Christmas times; and for a whole twelvemonth every one would look forward to the gathering together of the families. When they separated, they would agree upon the place of meeting for the next Christmas, and then try to wait with patience the rolling around of another year.

The place agreed upon for the gathering together at Christmas of a certain year, was the home of Mr. Larch who lived in the northern part of the county on a hillside farm.

The roads leading to it from the homes of the other two families came to a point about five miles south of it.

A triangle will illustrate the location of the three homes. Off to the north at the apex was Mr. Larch's, at the right of the base was Mr. Winterwood's, and at the left of the base was Mr. Walters'.

As the days grew on through December,

5

the young people of the latter two families could scarcely restrain their excited feelings, so joyously did they look forward to the journey on the ox sleds, and to the warm welcome that would await them at Farmer Larch's.

One of Mr. Winterwood's boys would awake each morning with the question, "Is this the day before Christmas?" and, being so often disappointed, at last went to bed saying he would sleep all through the days and nights until they could tell him it was the day before Christmas. But the time passed on, and Christmas drew nearer, slowly enough for the children, but faster for the grown people: for time moves with leaden pace for young, while he *flies* for those who begin to grow old.

At last it was the day before Christmas, and Willie Winterwood's question was no longer replied to with a "No." This time he received "Yes." Whereupon he turned two summersaults in the bed, struck his face against the bedpost, and had a black eye and a swollen nose for the rest of the week.   Nevertheless he was happy, although it is hard to *look* happy if your eye is blacked, and your nose swelled up to twice its proper size.

About ten o'clock, when they were to start, the leaden sky was full of snow, but the fine feathery particles had not yet begun to sift down upon the white blanket that already enveloped the earth.

The elders predicted a heavy storm, and doubted whether it was prudent to set out; out so doleful became the lamentations of the children that it was concluded to risk it anyhow.

I need not describe the packing of the sleds,—how the big baskets full of roasted turkeys and mince pies, and the crocks full of other good things were stowed away under the seats; nor how one of the boys was discovered on the front seat without his cap, which, in his eagerness to go, he had forgotten to bring, nor how one of Mr. Walters' little girls plunged headlong into a pot of butter, in her haste to find a seat. It isn't necessary either to describe the flutter and bustle and the shouting as the whips were cracked, and the cry arose: "Now we're off."

There were two sled-loads, drawn by two oxen each, starting from points ten miles apart, and expecting to meet at the junction of the two roads, when they would proceed in company.

The sled-loads were just alike, with this difference, that Mr. Winterwood's four children were all boys, and Mr. Walters' children were all girls. At Mr. Larch's there was rather a better division, for there were three boys and three girls.

Well, they have started, and we must imagine ourselves now up on the top of some high mountain looking down upon them as they move along. Off here to the right is Mr. Winterwood's party, off there to the left is Mr. Walters and his tribe, while away off beyond, eagerly waiting their coming, is the household of Mr. Larch.

The first mile or so of their way was as merry as it could be, but presently down came the snow. Such a snow as it was! It seemed to come down in shovelfuls. It was blinding—bewildering—be any thing.

The oxen became white—the folks in the sleds were piled around with it, and soon the roads became so heavy with it that the patient beasts could scarcely pull. But on and on they went, not however without many a dread on the part of the wiser of the parties that it would soon become so deep that they would be checked entirely.

At length, however, Mr. Winterwood's sled got as far as the junction of the two roads, where was a deep dark forest of hemlock-trees, whose wide-spreading branches spread out as umbrellas and kept off the heavy flakes; only a little white powdery snow could sift in over the brown carpet beneath the trees. It was a pleasant nook. The squirrels and the rabbits kept up a perpetual jollification there, and it was even reported that fairies had been seen dancing there in the moonlight, on summer nights. It was too cold that day before Christmas, however, for the fairies to be out; for you know their dresses are always *so* thin, and they wear no overcoats.

The tired oxen were glad to rest, and as for that, so were the people in the sled; even the impatience of the children was checked, and they were happy to scramble out of the sled, and be rid of the heavy blanket of white that completely covered them. Mr. Winterwood concluded to wait there for the arrival of Mr. Walters' sled. As they waited, the snow kept on falling faster and faster, as if the whole of some planet had been emptied out on the earth. [1.] By and by it began to grow late in the afternoon, and they were beginning to be afraid that Mr. Walters had turned back, when they heard some one calling, and presently the sled with its contents came in sight. It was hard to tell that it was a sled. It looked just like a great snowball moving slowly along. However, it was a real sled, drawn by oxen, and real people

were in the sled. But how tired they were!
I mean both the people and the oxen. They
had had a harder time than Mr. Winterwood's party, and were nearly used up. [2.]

Well, what was to be done? The snow
was drifting frightfully. Just beyond the
clump of trees, where they found shelter,
they could see the great banks of white,
covering up all traces of the road, and it
seemed too full of peril to attempt to floun-
der through it. But then what a disappointment to be only five miles away from where
they knew good cheer and welcome awaited
them, and yet to be unable to get any
nearer.

Some of the younger folks were for push-
ing on, for you must have imagined that
there were various Christmas gifts stowed
away somewhere among "the mince pies
and things," that they wanted to get out.
One of the little girls had a white kitten,
that wasn't among the mince pies however.
It was safely boxed up in the sled. It was
intended to be a gift to a small boy at Mr.

Larch's, and was now crying piteously. Poor kitten, it would have cried still harder if it could have realized what are the tender mercies of many a boy. That same kitten was subsequently found with a strip of red flannel tied to its tail, and harnessed to a wooden cart, trying, but trying ineffectually, to draw its master.

The elders, after going to the edge of the wood, and taking measurements in the snow, decided it to be too deep to go on, and that the night must be spent where they were. Possibly they could proceed in the morning when the snow ceased falling.

When this decision was reached, they all set to work to make themselves comfortable. Now it was a very different task, making themselves comfortable there, from what it was usually. But there is always a way when there is a will, so they took the blankets and buffalo robes, and with a framework of hemlock boughs soon had a rude tent made. It was a little too small, but it gave fine shelter to the two mothers, the babies, and the girls, while the men and boys leaned the sleds up against the trees, and found very fair shelter in that way. A blazing fire in front of the tent sent cut its genial warmth and thawed them out.

By and by they were very merry, and a great deal happier than they thought they could have been under such circumstances. The great big baskets containing their luncheon were brought out, and although they had to take snowballs instead of coffee or tea or milk, they had rather a good supper, and presently betook themselves to bed.

Now their beds, be it understood, were not fine mattresses nor warm feathers, but hemlock boughs. But what the beds lost in softness, they made up in fragrance; and every one slept tolerably well, although towards morning the boy with the swollen nose tried another summersault, and this time struck against a side of a sled and blackened his other eye.

When the morning dawned, the wind was moaning through the trees, but the snow had ceased. The sun presently arose upon as white a Christmas Day as was ever seen. All traces of the earth had disappeared, and it seemed as if the whiteness were intended to symbolize the purity of that Birth in the manger.

But although the snow had ceased, it was too deep to go on, and it seemed as if they must wait just where they were, and spend their Christmas in the woods.

Fortunately they had great mince pies they were carrying as gifts to Mrs. Larch, and quantities of other eatables were produced from the baskets.

There was no help for it but to devour the things they had intended as Christmas gifts.

Of course I do not mean the cat, for that was reserved for another fate. The appetites of the party were by no means diminished by their night in the woods, but steadily, steadily, the mince pies and the cold turkeys disappeared. It wasn't a bad breakfast either, even though they sat on the ground, and moistened each mouthful with a nibble of snow.

The children thought it the jolliest Christmas breakfast they had ever taken, and the older people thought it might do for a change, but they wouldn't like it as a steady thing.

After they had finished, Mr. Winterwood gathered them all together, and conducted a service for Christmas Day. It was a new way of keeping the festival of the Christ Child—there in the woods around a great fire. But their worship was none the less acceptable to the Babe of Bethlehem because it was not rendered in stately cathedral or in the sacred precincts of the Church. They were in God's temple,—a temple not made with hands.

The few simple carols they had learned rang out clear and full upon the wintry air; and a rabbit or two and a gray squirrel hearing the melody drew courteously near, and looked approvingly on.

The sober oxen as they munched the hay

that had fortunately been spread in the sleds,
seemed to the children to reproduce the cattle that once looked wonderingly on where a
Child lay in the manger of a stall. [3.]

There was a sermon too; a sermon not by
a clergyman, but by a layman; for when the
service was ended, Mr. Walters arose, and
this is what he said:—

"Dear ones all,—Here we are this white
Christmas morning snowed up in the woods,
but even here our hearts can be filled with
gladness, for we rejoice that the dear Lord
came down from heaven to be a little child
for us.

"Sheltered by these giant trees, we look
out upon the billows of snow yonder, and
think of the world that slept while in the
shed of a humble inn the virgin mother
pressed her babe to her bosom. The world
was as unconscious then, as the snow is now,
of the blessing that had come to men.

"Here we are shut in, while now in myr-
iads of places the echoing choruses of hymns
and psalms ascend to God in praise for His

best gift to men. But even here perhaps we are not alone, for it may be that in the solitude of this place there are heavenly visitants, the angels of the Lord, who are speaking good things to our hearts, and singing anew the anthem, 'Peace on earth, good-will to men.'"

That was the end of the sermon, but it was not intended to be the end.

He had a great deal more to say, but just at that instant, while all were listening intently to him, there arose an immense shout. [4.] What was it? Where did it come from? Who raised it?

Then it was repeated louder,—nearer.—

They sprang to their feet, ran in the direction of the sound, and what to their delighted eyes should appear but Farmer Larch with all his hired men, in a double yoked ox team.

They had been up ever since daylight, and had been breaking their way through the drifts, and had caught sight of the belated guests just as Mr. Walters was in the midst of his sermon. He never finished that sermon, but always declared that even though Mr. Larch and his hired men were not angels, their shout was an angel's shout, for it was good-will towards men.

Well, the noise that disturbed the Christmas sermon was nothing now to that with which the relief party was welcomed. Even the two quiet mothers with the babies raised their voices, and added to the din, when it was reported that the road was now clear.

The boy with the two black eyes and the swollen nose seriously contemplated trying another summersault, but he was caught in time to save his neck.

Well, they made a triumphal march of it. They left two sleds in the woods, harnessed the eight oxen in couples to one sled, and then all piled in.

It was a jam, but upon great occasions flesh and blood are very compressible. It was certainly so in this case. They all got in, and they all got out again, for the kitten had escaped, and the little girl whose treasure she was, was weeping bitterly. However, they soon found the pussy comfortably dozing by the dying embers of the fire, and she was captured, and relentlessly carried to her fate

Off they went. Why, it was the noisiest party that ever went over that five miles' road.

A poor little rabbit hearing the din, peeped out of a hollow tree where he had crept, but was so frightened that he drew in his head, and never looked out again until next day.

Two squirrels on a tree were so shocked that they tumbled over backwards into a deep snow bank, and never knew how they got there.

But it was the merriest Christmas Day that ever was spent, and young and old never regretted that they were belated Christmas guests in the woods along the Mohawk.

ROBERT ROUNCE'S CHRISTMAS.

ROBERT ROUNCE'S CHRISTMAS.

N the coast of Maine there is a
fishing village known as Winskogan.   It is beautifully situated,
but its inhabitants are, or rather
were, some years ago when this story opens,
of the roughest sort.   The men spent most of
the pleasant weather away from home fishing, and the long, cold winters were passed
around the stove of a miserable drinking
place known as Billy Brown's Bunk.

The women were an untidy set, addicted
to gossiping, quarrelling, and fighting.   The
children who grew up in the wretched homes
of Winskogan were any thing but attractive.
The highest ambition of most of the boys
was to become old enough to go with their
fathers to Billy Brown's Bunk, while the

girls were fast following in the footsteps of their mothers.

They were altogether as unpromising a set of children as could anywhere be found.

Strangers whom business called to the village made their way out of it as soon as they could, and no summer guests could be found to spend the summer months there, although there are few spots on the New England coast so thoroughly beautiful.

A graceful indentation in the shore line formed a bay, in the centre of which was an island covered with grand old trees. The beach was strewn with the finest white pebbles, while back of the village a gently sloping hill was carpeted in summer with the richest verdure. Beyond the hill was a lake of fresh water, abounding with fishes, and making a skating surface in winter as clear as crystal and as smooth as glass.

But the people of the place, intent only upon getting enough to eat, and indulging their debased natures, failed to enjoy the beautiful scenery, and they were so disa greeable as neighbors, that no visitors came among them except those who found it absolutely necessary, such as an occasional mer. chant to collect a bill, or a peddler to sell his wares.

Sunday was like any ordinary day in Winskogan, except that the fights and sprees were more frequent then than at other times. There was no church, and no minister ever visited the village, even for an occasional service.

Strange to say, however, in this debased settlement, where the name of God was rarely uttered, except in oaths and curses, and where all the influences were downward, there was one boy who was an exception to the others in many things. His name was Robert Rounce. Ilis parents were just like the other parents there,—just as unclean, just as neglectful of themselves, just as vi cious. Robert was fourteen years old when our story opens, fourteen in the early part of December. He was the leader of the boys in all their plays, but would never lead them

upon any of their thieving or fighting ex-
peditions. He was just as ragged and dirty
as they were, but they could never make
him lie or steal.

When they wanted a leader in some evil
doings, and such occasions were very frequent, they put Dick Lay at their head.
Dick was about as bad as a boy could well
be at sixteen. He could swear, and had
often fought in a ring.

These were the two leaders of the boys of
Winskogan. In all sports and games Bob
Rounce led them, but when there was a
plot to steal eggs, to sink a boat, or to have
a fight, they were led by Dick Lay. Perhaps it would be well to describe the personal appearance of the two boys. Bob was
of fair size for one of his years. He had
light hair and blue eyes, and when his face
was clean it was tolerably handsome. Seldom, however, was it clean. Generally it
was smudged and smeared, and his hair
hung in a tangled mass over his forehead.
His garments hung in tatters about him, and

were always too large for him, having first done service for his father. You might have seen him almost any evening in summer towards dark wending his way homeward with a pair of oars over his shoulder, or if it was winter he might have a big jack-knife in one hand, and a piece of wood in the other, industriously carving out the model of a ship. [1.]

If you saw him once you would know him again.

Dick Lay was a larger boy, broad shouldered, dark haired, and rather more ragged than the others. There was usually a frown upon his face, and nearly every one felt like giving him a kick or a blow, for if any thing was lost, or any one's pig was turned out of the pen, or any other mischief done, it was thought at once that Dick had a hand in it, or knew something about it. You would certainly not forget Dick's appearance after once seeing him. [2.]

About the beginning of one December the whole village of Winskogan was in a ferment. Three new families had arrived in this country from England, and, knowing the landlord of some of the houses in the village, had been induced by him to go and occupy three of his cottages that were vacant. The three fathers had been fishermen in the old country, and they overlooked the forbidding character of Winskogan in the prospect which they saw before them of earning a living by their nets.

The cottages of which they took possession were situated near the brow of the hill over-looking the lake. They had long been vacant, no strangers caring to live in so wicked a neighborhood.

These three families were good people, and members of the church. The children numbered in all nine girls and seven boys; a healthy, rugged party, fond of fun, but well trained and orderly.

The winter had set in cold and crisp when they came, and the children were soon busy with their skates and sleds on the pond, and as happy and as merry as children could be, except when they came in contact with the groups of boys who regarded their occupation of the pond as an intrusion.

Dick Lay proposed driving them from the pond altogether, but somehow or other "the little Englishers," as they were called, seemed so merry and so harmless that no one was quite ready to injure them, although they often were hooted at and worried.

From the day the children came, they were a complete fascination to Bob Rounce He would watch them by the hour at their sports, but for a long time no persuasion would induce him to come near them. He kept at a distance, and watched and admired, and when the other boys were rude would drive them back and stand guard over "the little Englishers." Gradually, however, their kind approaches overcame his diffidence, and he would now and then join them in their plays, but still he preferred standing off and watching them with admiring glances.

At length the day before Christmas came.

and there was great bustle and excitement in the cottages on the hill. The three mothers were busy preparing plum puddings, and the three fathers were just as busy pulling the feathers off the wild turkeys they had shot that day in the woods.

The children were huddling themselves up with cloaks and hoods and overcoats, preparing to go out to find Christmas trees.

Just as they were ready to start, one of them exclaimed—"Say, boys and girls, let's get Bob Rounce to go with us. He'll know where to find 'em." "Why," said another, "you can't get near enough to him. He's so shy." "Let's go down to his house anyhow" said a third, and so, laughing and chattering and skipping, on they went to get Bob Rounce. [3.] Presently they reached the cottage, knocked at the door, and heard some one inside call out—

"Come in, why don't ye?"

It almost frightened them, the tones were so gruff, but they mustered courage and went in. Faugh! how it smelt of fish, and tobacco

and whiskey. The smell nearly took their
breath. On one side of the fireplace was a
great tall man, seated on a stool, mending
a net. Bustling around, with a short clay
pipe in her mouth, was an ugly, coarse-feat-
ured woman. Two dogs raised their heads,
and growled at the children.

"What you want?—say," screamed the
woman.

"Please, ma'am," said little Julia, one of
the party, "we want Robert."

"Who's Robert?" cried the woman coming
towards them.

"Why, your little boy, ma'am; we want
him to go with us to get some Christmas trees," George, the oldest of the boys,
said.

"Ye mean our Bob, do ye? Well he's not
to home now. What's Krisnis trees? We
don't have any sich things as them here."

"Don't you," timidly replied one of them,
"why, we always had 'em at home, and we
can't just tell where to find 'em here, and
so we want your boy to go with us."

The woman looked at the children with strange surprise, and the man dropped his net on the floor.

Christmas trees! It was a new idea to them, but before they could have it further explained, the door opened, and Bob came in, blowing his fingers and slapping them on his breast to make them warm. When he saw the children, a broad grin spread itself over his face, but without a word he shrank into a corner, and looked at them with wondering eyes.

"See here, Bob," said his mother, "these here children wants you to git 'em some kind of a tree they calls Krisnis tree. I don't know nothing 'bout it; but jest you go with 'em and see wot it is."

Bob's cap was on his head in a moment, and with one bound he was out of the door, but there he stopped.

"Krisnis tree!" said he, "ain't got none here. Is it willers? Does yer want willers for to make baskets with?"

"No," replied one of the boys. "We want

some green trees to hang pretty things on,
and to light up. To-morrow is Christmas.
You go out to the woods with us and we
will show you what we are after."

Bob was never more perplexed in his life.
If they had asked him about boats, or fishes,
or nets, he could have told them any thing
they wanted to know; but Christmas trees!
Well, they were new to him; but the children
gathered around him, and their manner was
so kindly and their good humor so inspir-
ing that with a laugh he darted off towards
the woods, and the merry party after him.

Like one required to do something in the
dark, or like a bachelor asked to hold a
baby, Bob started away to the woods to find
Christmas trees; something green was all he
had in mind, and he knew that hemlocks
and cedars were green in winter.

His legs were swifter than the children's,
and the group that ran after him could hardly
keep up with him. [4.]

But when any one would tumble in the
snow, Bob would stop and help him up, the

broad grin of pleasure never leaving his face.
He had led many a party of dirty, rough
boys, but never had he been the leader of
such a merry, happy set.

We can not stop to tell the many strange
thoughts he had as he skipped along up the
hill, along the edge of the pond, down the
road, and across the fields to the great woods
beyond. Nor can we tell how he cudgelled his
brains to understand Christmas and Christmas trees.

At length, as they entered the woods, the
children screamed out,

"Oh, there they are. What beauties!"
and he saw them rush up to a great branch-
ing hemlock, and begin to lop off some of
the low branches.

In his eagerness to know what they wanted to do with these great green boughs, his
shyness vanished and he asked—

"Wot's it going to make. Yer can't
burn it."

"No, Bobby," one · answered, "we don't
want to burn the boughs, but we want them

for Christmas. That's to-morrow, and you
shall come, and see one of them all lighted
up, and trimmed with nice things. Don't
you keep Christmas too?"

"Don't know what it is," poor Bob con-
fessed.

The children's turn to be amazed came
now, for they never expected to see a boy
who really knew nothing at all about Christmas. One and then another poured into his
astonished ears the story of Christmas—how
Christ was born in a manger—how the angels sang on that blessed morning long ago
—how the shepherds left their flocks and
came to the manger—how the church bells
pealed forth their merry chimes every Christmas Day in their old home—and how they
used to sing carols in the old church at
home. Why they had so many things to
tell him that the poor boy's brain was all in
a muddle, and he asked if the angels grew
on Christmas trees, and if the church chimes
rang in the children's stockings.

It was a very merry walk home, each with

a good branch of hemlock on his shoulder. [5.] Even Bob had one, although he had no idea what to do with it when he got home or where he would put it. He was sure his mother would burn it up, or perhaps his father would cut off a big switch, and save it to whip him with.

By and by, as the little party reached the pond, one of them proposed that they should sing their old Christmas carols. "It will make the folks think of home," they said.

They paused a minute, and then out in the gathering twilight carolled forth the Christmas songs they had learned in old England. [6.] By the time they had finished singing two or three, the lights were lighted in the cottage windows, and the great fires within cast their ruddy glow over the group, making a picture of rare beauty. [7.]

"Good night," "Good night," "Thank you, Bob," "Come to-morrow and see the trees lighted up."

Bob started off home with his head almost bursting with the new ideas they had put

into it, and presently dashed into the hut
where he lived with the Christmas tree on
his shoulder.   Just as he expected, there was
a row about his bringing such a thing home.
"We ain't no room for it." "Out with it,"
his mother's shrill voice cried.   The poor fellow begged and implored that he might be
permitted to keep it, and then began the
most singular jumble of Christmas talk any
one ever heard.   He told his astonished parents about a Kris Kringle coming up out
of a stocking and filling a chimney with
candies and toys—about trees singing songs
up in the old church towers — about bells
lighted up with hundreds of lights—about
angels keeping watch over sheep—and shepherds flying through the air.

It was a curious jumble, but there was one
point he did get straight. He remembered
clearly about the One who was born in a
stable, and the gentle mother who cradled
Him in a manger, and in his own rough way
he tried to sing one of the carols he had
heard the children sing.

7

His parents thought the boy's wits were
leaving him, but when they saw his earnest-
ness and delight they felt something rising
in their hearts they had not known for many
a year, and before they went to bed that
night the rough father spoke more gently
than he had spoken for many a day. "Mol-
ly, 'pears to me I've hearn all that before
about the baby in the manger. My mother
used for to tell me suthin' like it afore I
comed to this here wild place. She used to
tell me suthin' like it, but it's putty much all
kinder knocked out of my head, only I 'member it was suthin' like that."

And there by the flickering firelight, the
rough man sat down, and tried to recall that
mother's words about the manger and the
babe. Did not some Christmas angel find his
way to that hut that night to assist the memory so clogged with the sins of later years ?
And did not some bright wing spread itself
out to give sweeter dreams to the poor boy
who that day had heard for the first time the
sweet, sweet story ? [8.]

What a day was that Christmas to Bob Rounce!

A light fall of snow had through the night covered the earth with a pure, fresh, white mantle. The clear, cold air was inspiriting. It was an ideal Christmas Day.

As the afternoon came on, and it was hard for Bob to wait for its coming, he might have been seen wending his way to the cottages on the hill.

It was evident that he had made some attempts at improving his personal appearance. His hair was combed, and his face and hands were some shades lighter. The rents and rags were still in his garments, but still he looked brighter and smarter. When he reached the first cottage the children saw him [9], and bouncing out hurried him in to the cheerful room where the fire burned so brightly, and where the very spirit of good humor freely abounded.

The first object that greeted his eyes was one of the trees he had helped them get, elevated upon a table, and covered all over with the prettiest toys he had ever seen. Some of them were the children's treasures saved up from the great Christmas trees in the old church at home. How the poor boy's eyes feasted upon the sight! So great was his delight that he gave a long, loud whistle, and whirled himself around and around, while his rags flew out like streamers on every side of him. And as he in this quaint manner expressed his joy, the children scampered about, clapped their hands, and laughed until the tears streamed down their cheeks.

But how shall we describe that happy afternoon? All the three families were gathered together in the same cottage and a merry time there was. They gave Bob some plum pudding, and so many other nice things to eat that his poor stomach must have wondered at the unusual food that was crammed down into it. Then they had some singing, and after awhile one of the fathers read the story of the Saviour's birth out of the Bible. After this came games and stories and long and happy talks.

Why, it was a new world for Bob, and his big eyes looked as if they would start forth from their sockets, while his ears drank in the pleasant things he heard.

It was his first Christmas. The day had come and gone for him thirteen times before, but never had he known what joy it could bring until now. His heart was thrilling with a new gladness.

When he went home in the pale moonlight, he scarcely knew whether he walked or flew, and sometimes he had to pull a piece of Christmas cake out of his pocket, and take a bite to see if he was not dreaming.

Was there ever such a delighted boy! Out of one pocket there stuck the end of a jumping-jack. The other was stuffed with cake. Around his neck was a string of candy toys, and in his cap one of the children had put some sprigs of evergreen. He was a perfect picture of gladness! As he got near home, he had to sit right down in the snow, to try his jumping-jack, munch his cake, and blow his tin trumpet. [10.]

Well, the days and weeks passed on, and with them came many changes. The new-comers to Winskogan were not content to have their neighbors remain in heathen darkness, and it was not long before a minister was engaged to come occasionally and preach the Gospel to them.

We will not describe the amazement of the fishermen as they flung themselves into the old boathouse where the first service was held, and saw the minister kneel to offer the first public prayers ever offered in Winskogan; nor need we tell how they listened to the first sermon which told them of the love of Christ for sinners.

Soon there was a Sunday school, and then a day school. Wonders of old time were repeated! Miracles seemed wrought again! Billy Brown's Bunk began to lose its customers, and ere long there wasn't a dog fight on Sundays in the whole village. Rags began to disappear, and people came out in clean, neatly-patched garments. Clean faces became the rule among the children, and a general brightening up spread over every one and every thing.

See what springs up there the next autumn!

Can we believe our eyes? They are actually building a chapel, and they say it will be ready at Christmas. The old boathouse is too small to hold the people, and they are hurrying on the chapel as fast as they can build it.

Day by day the work goes on! Hammering, sawing, painting, plastering! Yes, there it rises, a neat little building, and it will be ready by Christmas. Who could have dreamed of such a thing in Winskogan! But there it is, and prominent among the workers we see Bob Rounce. [11.] We hardly recognize him, so greatly has he changed. And who is that with him, carrying things for the workmen? Surely we know his face. Why, bless us, it is Dick Lay! [12.]

And now it is Christmas Eve again, and a happy group of children and older people are preparing the decorations of the chapel in Winskogan.

"The little Englishers" are there, directing hitherto untutored hands in the mysteries of trimming the evergreens about the windows, the arches, and the doors, and putting a glowing inscription on the walls. Bobby Rounce's father has remembered the story his mother told him so long ago. It is all fresh now, and he is here to help. His shrill-voiced wife has somehow or other toned down to a more modest pitch, and her shrill scream is seldom heard. She is helping too. Why, they are all helping! Great strong men, and as strong women, whom hardship and past excesses had once well nigh brutalized are there to-night, grown gentler, and, if we may judge by their eager interest to-night, they will welcome the glad Christmas morning with a joy they have never known before. But hark! The trimming has ceased. Sweet strains of music are float-

ing through the little chapel this Christmas Eve. [13.]   Hark! They are singing
a carol!   Louder and louder it grows as one
and another takes up the strain.

New voices have caught the melody.   Bob
Rounce and Dick Lay, and many more who a
year ago knew not the glad tidings, are now
singing with gladness this Christmas Eve.
We know not whether choirs of angels come
again to earth, but we can almost fancy as
these voices in the chapel stop their singing
that an angel host have taken up the old
song, "Glory to God in the highest, and on
earth peace, good-will towards men."   [14.]

HOW THE CREW OF THE SEA GULL SPENT CHRISTMAS EVE.

HOW THE CREW OF THE SEA GULL SPENT CHRISTMAS EVE.

UT on the ocean, on the day before Christmas of 1830, a sailing vessel known as "The Sea Gull," with canvas all set, was making her way swiftly towards the harbor of Harborport.

The voyage had been a profitable one, and now the crew were filled with happy thoughts of warm firesides at home, and hearty Christmas greetings from old friends and companions. They expected to cast anchor in the harbor early the next morning, and by the time the church bells were ringing, would, if all went well, go ashore, and join the Te Deum which they thought they could sing all the more heartily for their safe return from the perils of the sea. But as it grew towards dusk on that Christmas Eve, and when they were but a few miles from the harbor, a great blinding storm of hail and snow came rolling down upon them from the North, and blew them out to sea.

The sails were lowered, and for weary hours the vessel was driven by the wind they knew not whither.

It was a frightful storm and had come upon them almost without warning. The great flakes of snow came down upon the decks, and now and then a dash of hail would cut, as with knives, the faces and hands of those who had to stay on deck.

The wind whistled and moaned through the cordage and the cold waves fairly leaped over the vessel, as if they were pursuing fiends intent upon her destruction. [1.]

It was a night of terror. The best that could be done was to keep the vessel out of the trough of the sea, and trust to Him who holds the winds in the hollow of His hands.

Would the storm never cease? Would

there be no change? Where would they be driven to? Alas, they could not answer; and their hearts sank with disappointment as they thought of the homes to which they were once so near, but now were so rapidly leaving.

Dismay seized them as they found themselves driven so furiously onward, and as they thought of the perils of collision with other vessels, and of the possibility of being dashed upon some rocky shore.

But on and on went the ship, due southward, with the full force and swiftness of the storm. As if a giant had hurled her on, so went she in her headlong rush with the storm.

It grew so dark presently that they could no longer see the white snow, although it kept falling in heavy flakes mingled with the cutting hail. It was such a night of peril that the stoutest hearts among them began to lose hope, and to fear lest their Christmas should find them engulfed beneath the cold waves. They never expected to see the land again. But they were nearer the land than they supposed, for in the very height of the fury of the storm there was a crash that loosened every timber in the ship, and she was driven high up upon the beach of an island off the coast.

The ship staggered, and trembled, and then careened over upon her side, and there they were, somewhere, they knew not where, out of the depths of the sea among the breakers on the beach. Strange that they did not hear the breakers before, but then the din of the storm had been so loud, and their terror had been so extreme, that the breakers' roar had been unperceived, and beside no human skill or power could have changed their course. On the island they went headlong, and there they were.

When they had recovered somewhat from the shock, and had collected their scattered senses, they found the vessel beached far up where the water was not so very deep, and where upon the recession of the waves her bow was but a short distance in the

water. Expecting that she would go to
pieces, they concluded to get to the land
if possible. It was a difficult feat to do so,
but one by one they climbed out upon the
bowsprit, and watching their chance, at the
moment of the receding of the waves, they
swam and waded as best they could to the
shore.

Not a light was visible, and not a sound
except the roaring of the breakers, the rush
of the storm, and the whistling of the wind
through the shrouds of the deserted vessel.

They were on shore at last, and out of the
perils of the deep, but they were not much
better off after all, for all were wet, and cold,
the night was dark and not a place of shelter
could they find.

But they groped along, wearily climbed
over the line of sand hills that bounded the
beach, and at length stumbled into a deep
hollow in the sand where they were somewhat protected from the cold winds, and the
colder, cutting hail.

Here they huddled together and waited,

8

waited for what? They knew not what, only they waited; to keep themselves warmer, they dug with their cold fingers into the sand, and partly buried their bodies. It was but a poor device, but perhaps it kept them from perishing. [2.] But by and by came a change. They noted the gradual dying down of the storm. The blasts came less frequently and towards midnight there was a calm. The angry waves still kept up their roar, but the storm was over. It was however inky blackness all about them, save that here and there a star began to twinkle through a rift in the clouds. But they knew not where to go or what to do, and so remained huddled, and buried together in the hollow of the sand-bank.

After a time, one of their number raising his head fancied he saw a moving light landward. He told the others, and they stretched their necks, and peered in the direction he pointed out.

Sure enough it was a light, but what was it? See, there is another, and another, and now a score, moving along nearer and nearer towards them.

What are they? Who carry them? Is it a wrecking party of men with pirate-like feelings who have seen the wreck and come to plunder the helpless crew?

They can not tell, but at length resolve to get out of their sandy graves, and accost those who carried the lights.

As they straighten their stiffened limbs, and shake off the heavy wet sand that encumbers them, a burst of music reaches their ears—the words of an old carol which they had often sung at home in days gone by. They listen with perfect transport of joy, and when the chorus is reached raise their own weak, trembling voices, and join with all their might. [3.]

But what an effect their singing has had upon the party with the lights! They have ceased in terror, and with one accord have taken to their heels, and are rushing towards the village.

While the two parties are in this position,

I must pause and tell you who they were who carried the lights.

There was a fishing village on the island, numbering about two hundred souls; and for many years it had been the custom for the young fishermen to go around to the different cottages in the scattered village on Christmas Eve singing carols.

On this night of which I have been telling you, they were almost discouraged by the storm from following out their usual custom, and waited disconsolately in the cottage of one of their number until the midnight had come. But when they were about abandoning their intended serenade, and separating each for his own house, they found that the storm was over, and so were on their way to awaken the sleeping families with their bursts of Christmas music.

It was the first carol they had sung, when the chorus was so strangely taken up by the voices in the sand-bank.

Now you must remember that fishermen are usually superstitious folk, and when they heard the echo of their music from the voices in the bank, they at once concluded that the sea had rolled up its dead that Christmas Eve in the storm, and that the dead had joined the song of the living in honor of the natal day.

So did this conviction take possession of them that they expected to see the dead, with glassy eyes and shrunken features, but strangely endowed with life this Christmas morning, wrapped in the garments which the sea had wound around them as they rolled about in rocky caverns beneath the deep waters.

And so the carollers took to their heels and ran, heedless of the imploring voices the shipwrecked party sent after them.

It was a strange scene. The terrified singers hastening back to the village. The crew of the vessel following on as fast as their benumbed limbs would permit. One party shouting in terror; the other imploring them to stop and listen. [4.]

The noise they made finally aroused the

people of the village, and lights began to appear at one window and another. Here and there a door was timidly opened, and a head thrust out, inquiring, "What is the matter?"

At last, the carollers, as they reached the main part of the village, took up courage enough to turn and face the party whom they expected to find with ghastly countenances, and skeleton forms. But instead of meeting the dead, they saw the living. Instead of seeing frightful forms, they saw a party of men coated with sand,—feeble and wet and harmless.

All the previous terror of the fishermen now became changed to joy, when they saw that their superstitious fears were groundless, and that they had to deal with living men. It required but a few questions to understand the situation, and in the shortest time the whole village was aroused.

It did not take long to divide the shipwrecked party around among the warmhearted families of the island. It did not take long to build great blazing fires on the hearths. It did not take long to strip off the wet garments, and exchange them for dry ones, and to provide meat and drink for the hungry.

The Christmas morning had almost dawned before the excitement died down, and the village had sunken again to its wonted quiet.

Early in the morning, the bent form of the old clergyman who was the pastor of this secluded flock, was seen passing around from house to house to greet the new-comers, and to exhort them to thankfulness to God for their safe deliverance from the perils of the sea. [5.]

When the hour of service came, every seat in the little chapel was filled, and the choir in the organ gallery was augmented by the crew of the wrecked vessel. New gladness seemed to pervade every heart, and the service rolled on with deeper impressiveness, for the people seemed to welcome in the persons of the saved crew, the person of the Christ Child, who ever identifies Himself with

the suffering.   I wish I could describe to you
the singing on that Christmas morning.

There was no sermon, for the old clergyman said: "My friends, we will have no sermon to-day, for our carollers had a strange
interruption last night in their greetings to
Christmas Eve—and now they will have opportunity to finish.   Our brethren who have
been thrown into our arms by the sea, will
help them make melody unto the Lord."

Then for a whole hour that old wooden
chapel rang with the music of old time
Christmas carols.   [6.]   Why, it was a very
feast of music.   No one stopped to consider
how artistic it was, but there was a depth
and tone to it all that made the simplest of
their songs almost entrancing.

Why was it so?

Simply this—the rescue of a few men from
the jaws of the mighty deep impressed them
all with the mightiness of the greater rescue
which He accomplished who became man,
and saved us from the death eternal.

AUNT KITTY'S CHRISTMAS TREE

AUNT KITTY'S CHRISTMAS TREE.

VERY body called her Aunt Kitty, although in truth she wasn't any body's aunt, at all, for she had not a relative in the world. But she was so good and so kind that any one would have thought it an honor to have claimed kinship with her. She was very poor and very old. The old age she could not help, that had to come; but the poverty she might have helped, if only she had been a little bit dishonest. Yes, at the time her husband died, she had the opportunity to save some of the wreck of his property. Some of her advisers told her just how she could conceal it, and the creditors would have been none the wiser. But she gave up every fraction of it, and went out into the world to seek her own living in her old age, poor, but with no taint of dishonor. She had resisted the great temptation, and her conscience was free from reproaches.

Few of the people in the village of Bland-stone knew her past history. They only knew her as a poor old body who went out sewing, and taking care of sick folks. She rented two rooms in a house on a back street, at one end of the village, in a neighborhood where every one was nearly as poor as she was, except that some went into the struggle for bread with greater strength than she. But to none of them was the daily bread given by "Our Father in heaven" more unfailingly than to her. She trusted Him, and He saw that she was fed. Now and then she had more than she needed, and some poor, sick sufferer would be helped from her supply.

Of course she was a great favorite in the place. Many a one would gladly have offered her a home with them, but she preferred keeping her own rooms and her inde pendence, and thus it happened that she lived alone. Not entirely alone, for there were two big cats that purred contentedly beneath her stove, or slept in the sunny windows. [1.] Now and then, some wanderer, some child or woman, would find a shelter in her house, for a few days, to be warmed and fed and sent on rejoicing. It was strange how the wanderers found her out, but they did. If a poor widow was on her way to the city to collect a pension, she was almost sure to find shelter with Aunt Kitty. If some young girl was hunting a place to work, she would make her home with Aunt Kitty until she found one.

Many were the blessings which were supplicated upon her head, and if she did not enjoy them all here, perhaps they await her yonder. Although she had no children of her own, she was the friend of all children. They stopped their plays to speak to her,— they brought their cuts and burns to her to be bound up—and many a torn jacket and breeches did she mend that the young culprits might not be punished at home for rents that come so mysteriously, but come so certainly, in a boy's clothes.

There were some pretty rough boys too in that part of the village, but somehow she had reached their hearts, perhaps through their stomachs, and they were her loyal friends. Many a quarrel among them did she stop, and many a damaged eye did she bandage when the fights were over which she had failed to stop.

Aunt Kitty got a new idea one day as December was hastening on to Christmas-tide. All at once it occurred to her that she would have a Christmas tree for the poor children of that street.

Now Christmas trees are usually costly affairs when they are all trimmed, as we generally see them. But her tree could not be a costly one. It must bear very inexpensive fruit. If her purse had been larger she would have made it a very beautiful tree, or if she had asked any of the church people of the village they had helped her, but she wanted to do the best she could with what she had, and so she kept the whole matter to herself, as she thought, a profound secret. Not even the boys were to know about the tree until Christmas really came.

The poor old hands were wonderfully busy during those two weeks before Christmas. Little pieces of bright materials, the remnants of dresses she had once worn, somehow grew into dolls and dolls' clothing. Out of an old chest she fished up a few pictures and toys which had long lain there undisturbed. A few little purchases at the village shop added to the treasures she was accumulating. Then the smell of baking indicated that gingerbreads in wondrous shapes were being made ready. It was hard to satisfy the inquisitiveness of the small visitors, whose noses scented the appetizing odors, and who wanted to know what Aunt Kitty was cooking. But no satisfaction could they get. Aunt Kitty had a secret, and she was keeping it, she thought, all to herself, and

was preparing a grand surprise for the dozen
boys and girls who were her neighbors.   [2.]
But isn't it hard to keep a secret?   And isn't
it strange how they will leak out?   And are
not people very shrewd in putting this and
that together and guessing a great deal?

While the old woman was stitching away
at dolls and baking gingerbreads, there were
three boys who were just as busy planning,
and circumventing the scheme which she
had been laying out. Perhaps we ought
not to say that they were circumventing
her scheme; it is true their putting their
heads together was going to make a change
in it, but we will see how it was presently.

These three boys were brothers, one was
big, another was little, and one was neither.
They were the sons of a wealthy widow lady
who lived in the heart of the village, and
were all three of them trying to be a comfort
and a joy to their mother. They were choristers in the choir of the church, and it
seemed to give a greater depth to their
mother's devotion as she heard their voices

singing week by week in the church services. One day as one of them was in the village store buying a new top, and talking with the queer old man who sold the odd things kept there, Aunt Kitty came in, and with a very mysterious air bought a few toys which she tried in vain to conceal from the sharp eyes of Clarence Wood.   [3.]

"Now what can she want with toys?" thought Clarence. "She don't need them for herself. What is she going to do with them?"

Now nothing can exceed the curiosity of a boy, so all the rest of that day he wondered what Aunt Kitty could be intending to do with those toys. When it became night he told his brothers, John and Frank, and they made up their minds to find out if they could. After many plans had been proposed and discussed they resolved to take up a bag of chestnuts and some apples to Auntie the very next day, and see what she was really going to do with the toys.

They suspected that she had some good

project afoot, and already the desire was springing up in them to help her on with it. . [4.]

But to all their questionings she returned indefinite answers, and they started to go away unsatisfied, but just as they were leaving the door they caught sight of the end of a great bunch of cedar peeping out of the cellar window.

"Aha, I see now," said John. "Aunt Kitty is going to have a Christmas tree." And so they ran home, and set to work as hard as they could to get things ready for that Christmas tree, for they said as they went along—"Let us make it a real jolly tree. It must be for the poor children, and we'll have a hand in it."

They told their mother, and a few others, and as if by magic great heaping baskets were filled with all sorts of things.

But as yet they did not know when it was to be, nor how they could get at it. But they were shrewd fellows, and kept their eyes open

Finally, on Christmas Eve, they strolled along down by Aunt Kitty's house, and saw that both rooms were lighted up. In the lower room a dozen or so of boys and girls were sitting around, and in the upper room they could just distinguish through the white curtain the outline of the Christmas tree on a table near the window.

"I have it," said Clarence, "we'll run home, get the things, put them on the tree, and then see how the frolic will end."

So back they went, got the baskets and a ladder, hurried again down the village, and began operations. It was a very delicate operation, climbing up into the second story, but the house was low, and they had the satisfaction of getting in without making any noise. [5.] They could hear the children chattering down-stairs, and just as they had fairly laden the poor tree with the many things they had brought, they heard Aunt Kitty say, "Now, children, I'm going to take you up-stairs to show you something that you all will like to see." The boys up-stairs

hastily concealed themselves in a closet among
the dresses hanging there, and had just time
to do so, as Aunt Kitty came in, with the
children flocking after her. Now you must
remember that when the good old auntie
had last seen the tree it was almost bare.
The few things she had been able to make
ready were by no means enough to cover
its many branches. But now what a change!
It was fairly loaded down! Caps and scarfs,
gloves and stockings, dolls and skates—why,
almost every thing you could think of was
fastened to it.

With an exclamation of surprise, as great
as that the children themselves raised, she
ran to the table.

Who had been in her room? Who had
brought these things? Was there really a
Santa Claus? [6.]

And there she stood amazed. Her senses
seemed to have deserted her. She thought
it all a dream, but the noisy shouts of the
children roused her to herself, and she said;
" Dear children, I can not tell how it is. I

made ready a few things for you, but the good Lord in some strange way has sent all this."

What else she would have said no one knows, for just at that moment, bang went something against the closet door, and out rolled Clarence on the floor. He had not been able to contain his mirth, and in a fit of laughter had leaned too hard against the door, and open it came, rolling him out on the floor. [7.]

Auntie saw through the plan now at once, and, although she had been frightened at first, she added very calmly, "Yes, the good Lord has sent the things, and these are his agents."

Well we need not stop to tell how the culprits gained her pardon for getting into her house, nor what a happy time there was in distributing the gifts. There was a rich abundance for all the children, and many a comfort for the good auntie herself.

But another surprise was in store for them all, and this time the three boys were as much surprised as the rest, for after the last of the gifts had been distributed, they came down-stairs to find it filled with some of the good people of the village who had quietly come in, bringing baskets laden with good things. There were groceries, and wood, and new dresses, and a warm cloak. Why, Aunt Kitty was quite fitted out for the long winter. [8.]

With the tears streaming down her eyes, she said to her unexpected guests, "The Lord bless you all for your kindness, and may the dear Christ make you all as happy as you have made me."

REUBEN REUBENSON'S CHRISTMAS EVE.

REUBEN REUBENSON'S CHRISTMAS EVE.

EUBEN REUBENSON was a cross, crusty bachelor, who had somehow managed to reach his fiftieth year in selfishness and solitude.

He claimed kinship with no one living, and no one cared particularly to claim kinship with him.

He was rich in this world's goods, but beyond managing his bank accounts, and keeping a sharp eye upon some property interests, he had no business.

Neither had he any settled home, but floated about from place to place as his own capricious fancy prompted him.

Now he was here—now he was there.

Why he was here rather than there, or why he was there rather than here, it would have puzzled any one to tell. Sometimes he himself could not tell. The slightest reason was sufficient to make him change his abode. A disagreeable rainy spell, the sight of some poor cripple, an appeal for help, a crying baby, a badly prepared dinner, would lead him to pack up his trunk and move off.

Owing to these frequent changes of residence, few people knew him well, although his face and his oddities were well known to many, and they spoke of him as the queer, unhappy old man, who was always on the wing.

For a few weeks before a certain Christmas season, he had been spending his time very quietly, and, for him, very comfortably, in a pleasant boarding place in the town of Ross; but his comfort was utterly destroyed by the arrival of some Christmas guests at the house where he was staying.

These guests were the country aunts and cousins of the keeper of the boarding-house, and had come to see the sights and to spend a merry Christmas together.

They brought with them a baby, a blessed baby. Now it has been said that a babe in the house is a well-spring of pleasure; but this baby did not prove to be entirely so. It was one of those irrepressible creatures with strong lungs, and he knew how to use them.

Without any warning by previous whimpers of discontent, gradually rising by a crescendo movement to a generous volume of sound, this baby was capable of uttering his howls of protest *suddenly*, savagely, and of prolonging them until almost all memory of other sounds was obliterated, and there seemed to be nothing vocal in all the world but that one red-faced creature.

Mr. Reubenson had no sooner heard one of the shrill, startling yells, then he began to pack up his trunk to go.

In vain the landlady protested against his leaving. No arguments, no appeals, could induce him to change his mind. Go he would.

She offered to change his room, to send

the baby home as soon as she could, but it
was all of no avail. Even her offer to admin-
ister sedatives, *ad libitum*, to the baby fell
upon deaf ears, and at length, growing out
of all patience with her boarder, she declared
that she had offered to do every thing except
to strangle the child, but she had not promised that, for she thought if any one stood
in need of strangling, it was Mr. Reubenson
himself.

Now, putting things as mildly as possible,
this was rather a savage remark to make,
even to a crusty old bachelor; and it hastened very greatly the packing of his trunk.

Before another hour he was on his way to
the railway station. When he reached there,
he was all uncertain which route to take.

There had been an accident a short time
before on the Black Creek R. R., and his fears
would not let him go over that route. On
the Lake Shore road he had once been greatly disgusted at the conduct of an official, and
hence that way was out of the question.

In very desperation he concluded to try a

new road which had just been opened, although with the country through which it ran he was entirely unacquainted.

However there was no choice now, so finding a train about ready to start, he pulled out his pocket-book, took from it a bank-bill, and resolved to buy a ticket for as far as that bank-bill would carry him.

It was an odd way to select one's place of destination, but he was an odd man.

The ticket agent took the bill, and as saw its amount said interrogatively, " want to go to Brierake?"

"What is the fare?"

"Just right," was the reply, and the ticket was received.

Now Mr. Reubenson knew about as much concerning any place called Brierake as he did of the mountains in the moon. It might have been a country village, it might have been a cross road's station, for all he knew; but "all aboard" shouted the conductor, and our traveller started for Brierake, little dreaming of the strange incidents that awaited him

at the end of his winter's journey, or of the
great change that would come over him before he came back.

The day passed as most winter days pass
in railway cars. The short afternoon had
faded away and the early evening was creep-
ing on when he was landed at Brierake
station.

There was little of the village or of any settlement whatever to be seen. A plain, un-
painted station-house, a heavy, awkward sled
drawn by two sleepy horses muffled up in
their blankets, a queer-looking teamster, and
an old woman with a market basket and the
inevitable bandbox—these were the objects
that met his gaze. Upon inquiring of the
teamster, he learned that the village itself
was some three miles away, and that the
only way to get there was by taking passage in the sled. He would have grumbled
if he could have seen any use in grumbling,
then and there, but it is dull work to grum-
ble on the platform of a way station on a
cold winter's evening, so he mounted the

seat of the sled, pulled up the collar of his overcoat, wrapped around his knees the old, torn buffalo robe which the driver handed him, declined the offer made by the old woman with the bandbox to take a pinch of snuff—and then resigned himself to what he thought would be a dreary three miles ride.

But it wasn't dreary at all. The horses awoke from their sleep at the cheery call of the driver, and dashed off smartly with visions of oats and hay and a warm stable before them. The bells jingled merrily. The moon began to rise and flood the earth with a silvery beauty. Presently a turn in the road revealed a most lovely landscape. The fields and road covered with snow, and a green border of tall cedars. The traveller found his spirits rising with every inch of the way, and did what was for him an exceedingly gracious thing: he asked the old woman by his side if she were warm enough.

She was a garrulous old body, and the simple question put to her launched her forth

into an extended account of herself and all
her family, which account went on and on
and on, and seemed to promise no ending.
But tedious as would have been her talk at
any other time, Mr. Reubenson found himself listening to it with respectful attention.
What spell was coming over him that he
could thus patiently listen so long to an old
woman's story?

Presently they came to the bank of a little
frozen stream, over whose slippery surface a
merry group of skaters were gliding with
graceful movements and cheery shouts.

So charming was the picture they thus
presented in the moonlight that he was
almost on the point of asking the driver to
stop awhile that he might enjoy the scene;
but now the lights of the village beyond began to flash forth, and the horses went dash-
ing on faster and faster, until before he realized it they had drawn up in front of an old
inn—one of the quaintest hostleries he had
ever seen.

Its parts seemed joined together in a rambling sort of way without any particular design, but betwixt the ruddy lights from its windows and the moonbeams which streamed upon it, and the white snow which covered its roof and sheds, it bore no small resemblance to a place of enchantment.

It could not be called an enchanted palace, nor could Reuben Reubenson be called the prince who had come to awaken the sleepers. It was only an old inn upon a winter's night, brightened up by moonlight and firelight; and he was only a crusty old bachelor whom some good influence, what it was he could not tell, was thawing out, and making more mellow and more sweet than hitherto.

It is needless to describe how the hungry man devoured the supper so quickly spread for him, or with what comfort he ensconced himself in the great arm-chair before the fireplace in which there was blazing a wood fire large enough to roast an ox, provided the ox was not very large.

There he sat and watched the flames

Presently the fire as it crackled and darted out its long tongues, and danced before him, seemed wondrously suggestive of just such a chimney-place where he had sat many years ago, when he was one of a happy family of brothers and sisters in a far-off home. And he mused of the days so long gone, and of the forms which had been warmed at the fire of that old home.

What had come over him to so unlock the memories of the past? For years he had sealed up these recollections, and by strong effort of will had remanded them back; but now how he welcomed their coming!

His thoughts grew so busy with the past that he peopled again the chimney-place with the departed, and it was as if he were home again. Now a tear went stealing down his cheek as he recalled the joy of that home, and now his lips opened as if he would speak to those who had sat there long ago with him. [1.]

The hours sped by, and still he watched the fire, and thought of the past, until just as he was falling off into a sleep there came a burst of music. [2.]

It startled him. He jumped up from his chair. Where could it have come from?

And in his bewilderment he stopped to see if the chimney were really alive, or if the crackling fire upon the hearth had become melodious in honor of the nearing festival. But soon the music grew louder and clearer, and presently there rang out in joyous notes the sweet voices of a score or so of young people in the street outside singing their Christmas carols. [3.]

Now Reuben Reubenson ordinarily had but little ear for music. Once he had, but he had let the sweet sounds within him die out, and even children's voices had become but a worry to him. But to-night he had passed into a strange region. He had been led, he scarcely knew how, and the spell of the place and of the time was upon him. He listened greedily, especially as he thought that the tones of the voices were wondrously like those of his own brothers and sisters in the home of long ago. Carol after carol rang forth upon the crispy air. [4.]

Such exuberance of joy, such unrestrained gladness he had rarely heard thrown into songs before. They seemed to renew his youth, and to melt off the icy crust of selfishness which had gathered with his manhood.

The carol singers outside, all unconscious of the effect of their singing, only thinking of the gladness of the festival, uttered forth their joy that the Christ was born of Mary in David's town. [5.]

Presently they passed away, still singing.

The sound of their voices grew fainter and fainter, until they seemed as a gentle lullaby which a mother might .sing over her sleeping child. [6.] And as a lullaby did the vanishing sounds become to him, for beneath their soothing influence he sank to sleep.

But it had been strange if one so moved as he had been had slept soundly that night in his chair before the fire.

His body only seemed unconscious, while a thousand recollections rushed through his busy brain. He seemed to be living over again his boyhood days, waiting with boyish impatience the coming of Christmas Day. He saw himself as a boy lying awake upon Christmas Eve in his bed in the old home, hoping, yet dreading, that he might see Santa Claus come down the chimney.

Then he seemed to be again one of the merry group of children whose delighted eyes looked upon the Christmas tree laden with its strange stores of wonderful fruit. [8.]

Then he thought himself again at church in England, and heard the old hymn, "O come all ye faithful," which he and the other choristers sang as they marched up the long aisle of the church on Christmas mornings. [9.]

And as he dreamed on there, how real it all seemed—those happy boyhood days before he had grown up to a selfish manhood; but his mind travelled on, and in his dreams he saw himself leaving his home to better his fortunes, and with bettered fortunes losing the impressions of home, and forgetting the holy things he had learned.

He watched the gradual growth of selfishness, and the dying out of the spring and
hopefulness of early manhood, until there
arose before him a picture of what he was
then, that Christmas Eve, a cold, ice-bound,
self-indulgent man, with no aims and no
hopes.

It was a repulsive picture, and yet he was
under the influence of some power that made
him look upon it in all of its repulsiveness.
And as he looked, so painful did the view become, that he awoke with a start from his
dream to find the fire growing low on the
hearth, and himself shivering with cold and
with dread of the horrible picture his dreams
had brought to him.

There was no more sleep for him all the
rest of that long winter's night. He paced
the floor and thought. He knelt down by
his chair and prayed. He buried his face in
his hands and wept. Then he resolved that,
through the grace of God, he would be a
better man. He thought of the children who
had sung their carols before his window, and

longed to be as happy and as innocent as they. Then he began to plan what he would do to make amends for thirty years of selfishness and neglect—how he might give back to God some portion of a life which should all have been God's—how he might break through the icy bands which froze his sympathies up from his fellow-men and help along the echo of the angels' song—"Glory to God—peace, good-will to man."

It was a memorable night in the history of Reuben Reubenson. The hours sped along, but he heeded neither the darkness nor the cold. His mind was too busy.

His heart was too deeply stirred. His one great yearning was for pardon for the past, and for God's blessing for the future that he might end his days making others happy.

"I will have an aim in living and it shall be a noble one. So help me God," he said.

What a bright Christmas morning was that which dawned! The stars went out one by one, as lamps no longer needed, as the day began.

The gray tints touched the hill-tops, and then the red tints of the rising sun bathed the snow in crimson. [10.]

Presently the soft, low tones of a bell fell upon his ear, announcing that pious souls were assembling to greet the Christmas morning with holy rites and hymns and prayers.

Passing forth from his room, he followed the sound of the bell, and found himself in the little chapel whose interior was bright with the adornments of evergreen which busy hands had grouped around arches and windows.

Not a soul did he know there among those who had come to worship, and yet he felt that he would meet his Lord there to Whom his vows had been renewed that Christmas Eve.

None knelt more reverently in prayer to Him who had come into the world a little child, who had taught men the beauty of self-sacrifice and the glory of a holy life.

To none of the worshippers was bestowed so large a measure of grace, for the battle Reuben Reubenson was to fight was with himself. It was to be against the long years of hardness and selfishness, and he needed especial help from God.

When the service was over, and the minister was counting over the offerings which had that morning been presented, there was found among them in the alms-basin four one hundred dollar bills, new, and crispy in their newness, wrapt up in a leaf torn from a memorandum-book.

Upon the leaf was written in a tremulous hand with pencil these words:—"An offering to God for his goodness in leading me, partly through the sweet voices of the children of this place, to see the folly of a life of selfishness. And in further token of my desire to spend the remainder of my days to the glory of God and for the welfare of men, I promise to contribute a like amount each year, to be employed in training the children of this church to sing hymns and carols at Christmas-tide, and in any other way the minister may think best to keep young hearts from the icy bands of selfishness which so long held sway over me."

The paper was signed—

"REUBEN REUBENSON."

THE MIDNIGHT CHIMES.

THE MIDNIGHT CHIMES.

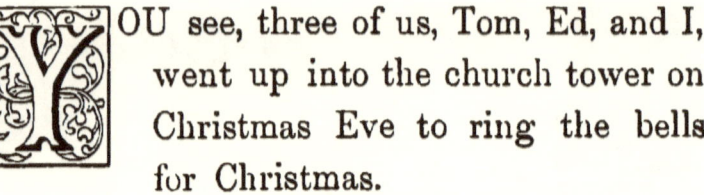OU see, three of us, Tom, Ed, and I, went up into the church tower on Christmas Eve to ring the bells for Christmas.

It was about a quarter of an hour before midnight when we went up.

There wasn't a soul about when we entered the church. It was lively work ringing the bells, and we pealed out carol after carol for nearly an hour, until we thought if we were to be in church again that morning we ought to get home and go to sleep. When we came down the tower stairs Tom was carrying the lantern. Just as he got to the last step, says he, "Let's look in the church and see if the folks finished putting up the greens."

As he said this he turned the bull's-eye
of the lantern towards the chancel, but instantly he jumped back.

"What's the matter?" I said.

Says he, "See there! Bless me, if it ain't
a man or a ghost!"

"Pshaw!' Ed says, "guess you're sleepy
and dreaming. Else you've seen your own
shadow."

Well, we stood there till Tom made his
lantern brighter, and sure enough there was
a man lying down on the floor, way up near
the front of the church. I tell you now I
felt rather queer over it. How did he get
in? What did he want?

There was no use standing looking, so we
plucked up courage and walked up, keeping
pretty close to each other. Was he asleep?
Was he dead? He was lying on his face
with his hands stretched out before him. I
thought he was dead, but Tom shook him
by the shoulder, and he slowly raised his
head. He was a young fellow like one of
us, but he was awful weak and sick-looking.

"What are you doing here?" I asked.

All the answer he gave was a groan, and down went his head on the floor again. Well, we tried to rouse him up, but he seemed to be in a fainting fit; and Ed thought we had better sprinkle water over him, or do something. But you see we didn't know what to do, and we couldn't find any water. And there we stood around the young fellow in the church, early that Christmas morning. The bull's-eye lantern seemed to make the shadows of the arches jump around as if they were alive, and the evergreens the ladies had put up, made it seem awful odd. I declare, I wished I was home and in bed, and made up my mind that there were a great many things pleasanter than finding a strange man in a fainting fit on a church floor, early on Christmas morning.

Something had to be done, so we picked him up and carried him over to the hospital, and left him there. When we came away, the doctors were rubbing him, and forcing medicine down his throat, but he couldn't speak yet, and we don't know who he is, or what he wanted. His pockets were empty, and his clothes were pretty well worn out. He did not look like a hard drinking fellow, but he appeared to have seen hard times for a young chap.

And that's all I know about it.

II. THE DOCTOR'S STATEMENT.

Early on Christmas morning, just after I had fallen to sleep again after having been wakened up by the ringing of the Christmas chime, there came a tremendous rapping at the hospital door, and I hastened down to see who was there. I found three young fellows, who had been ringing the church bells, supporting an emaciated man evidently not over twenty-five years old, who seemed to be in a condition of great exhaustion. They had found him in the church.

After a thorough examination, I found no wounds or evidences of disease. He seemed to be simply worn out by hunger, fatigue, and trouble. It was a long time before I could induce him to speak, but towards day dawn he seemed to rouse up a little, and looking wildly around exclaimed:

"The Christmas Bells! Thank God!"

For some hours after this he remained in an insensible condition, and then began slowly, but steadily, to regain strength. He maintained silence as to his antecedents for a long time, but expressed great gratitude for our efforts in his behalf. At length, just as the bells began to ring for the services on Christmas Day, he seemed to be greatly agitated, and at my urgent solicitation, gave me an outline of his story. It was a sad story.

He was of good family in England, but owing to a quarrel, or some difficulty which he had had, he suddenly left home for the new world. Reaching here, a course of dissipation soon used up his means, and after begging his way from village to village, he reached here on Christmas Eve nearly ready to die and finding the church door open, crept in, and was found there by the bell-

ringers, as they have described. He has prepared the following message, which he has
entreated me to send by the cable at once
to his home in England: "Mother and Mary,
come! Saved from ruin and death by the
Christmas Chime." I am on my way now
to send it, and he is to stay here until an
answer is received.

III. THE PATIENT'S STORY.

I have told the kind doctor only part of
my eventful history, but how can I longer
refuse to tell him all? He has gone with
the telegram that will summon to me the
two whom I love best in all this world.
Ah! how now I realize my love for them,
and also my deep ingratitude! A year ago
my prospect in life so bright that I was one
of the happiest of men. My studies were
completed and I was on the point of being
admitted to the bar, but in an evil hour I
was led into temptation, and in less than
six months had contracted the habit of in-
toxication. I recall now the anxiety and

tears of my mother, and the bitter grief of the dear wife to whom I had plighted my troth.

Going home one night in a condition bordering closely upon delirium, their gentle expostulations roused the demon within me, and I struck them both. My gentle mother and my loving wife! Oh, I could cut off the hand that gave the cruel blows. I knew not what else I did, but as the morning broke, and as I awoke from sleep, the sense of shame so overwhelmed me that I crammed hastily into my valise a few articles of wearing apparel, made my way to the nearest port, and took a steamer for America. On the voyage my conscience lashed me so that it seemed there would never be any way to quiet its reproof. I shunned the company of my fellow-voyagers, and in a condition of alternate stupor and delirium got somehow through the weary days.

I reached Boston without plans or aims, and in a condition of desperation. There I was, an utter stranger. It was early in December, and the weather was growing bitter cold. I could not rest in any place, but roamed from town to city, spending whole days and nights in dissipation, until at length my money gave out and I became a beggar. Yes, a beggar! I, the son of affluence, with wealth at home, begged my bread from door to door. I could not work, I cared not to work. Spending my days in plodding along the frozen highway, stopping now and then at a farmhouse to get a morsel to keep me from starving, and sleeping in barns and cattle sheds, the year drew towards its end, and I saw everywhere the preparations for Merry Christmas. How the sight of the joy of others maddened me! I knew that at home there would be but little joy in one house which my sin had darkened. I knew that for the first time since my father's death my poor old mother would find her son's place vacant at the table, and my young wife would recall the happiness of past days when we had kept the festival together. Christmas Eve found me on the highway.

I was tired, hungry, and well-nigh distracted. The wintry winds blew keenly, and I thought I would freeze but for the maddening fever that kept my brain on fire. On and on I walked. I had no thought of stopping to rest. No thought but to .go on and on. At last I saw the lights of a town, and they were few and far between, for it was well on towards midnight, and the bustle of the evening had quieted now. Here and there I saw a lighted window, and peering through the windows saw them making preparations for the morrow.

But hurrying on, I came to a bridge over a swift stream. The moon was rising,. and although I was so absorbed in my own mournful thoughts that I scarcely saw the planks of the bridge, I noticed just over the edge, one place where the ice had not formed. There was a swift eddy whirling round and round. Somehow it fascinated me. I stopped to look. Hands that beckoned me seemed to be stretched out of the water. Instantly the thought of suicide entered my brain! I had

never thought of it before, but now it took
possession of me. There was the opening
in the ice just over the edge of the bridge.
I walked to the railing and mounted it, ready
for the fatal spring.

I had no other thought than self-destruc-
tion—but at that very instant, just as I was
poising myself to leap into the water, the
bells in a neighboring church pealed forth a
merry Christmas carol, and the clocks of the
town struck twelve. Christmas had dawned.
I was saved! The demon hands in the water
seemed to sink out of sight, and I sprang
back again to the roadway of the bridge,
shuddering at the awful crime I had been
on the point of committing.

I rushed on over the bridge. Some impulse, I know not what—was it not a guar-
dian angel?—led me on and on down the
street to the church from whose tower there
were pealing forth sweet strains of music. I
stopped now and then to listen. They were
playing the same old carols we used to sing at
home. What a flood of memory they brought

back? In a little while I reached the church. I had no thought of entering it, but behold, the door was ajar, and I went in. It was all dark within, and without knowing why I did so, I groped my way along towards the chancel, up the broad alley. I could see nothing, it was so dark; but I could feel the warmth of the fires, and could smell the odor of the hemlock boughs with which the arches were decked.

Slowly groping my way along, I reached the chancel step. My foot struck against it, and I fell forward on my knees. I did not intend to kneel there to pray. I fell there, or rather God's angel put me there, and as I raised my eyes, the moon which had been rising, had reached a point whence her beams shone suddenly through one of the pictured windows of the chancel. It was like a vision from heaven! Upon that window was the full length representation of the merciful Christ. What tenderness was in His face —what pleading love! I could not resist the impulse to cry out—

"Lord, have mercy upon me a sinner!"

The fountain was unsealed. Never before in my agony had I thought of pardon, but new hope sprang up as I looked upon that pictured window and thought of Him whose mercy and love it shadowed forth. From the very depths of my soul I prayed. I know not what words I said, nor how long I remained there. At intervals I could hear the chime still ringing, but presently its sounds became fainter and fainter. I thought I was dying, and with one last effort of strength, stretched out my hands towards heaven, and knew nothing more until I awoke here.

Blessings, rich blessings, rest forever upon those whose benefaction placed that chime of bells in the church tower. Blessings upon those who rung them that Christmas morning, for had it not been for the sweet carol that floated out at midnight, I had been a suicide.

And now, if strength be given me, I must undo the evil I have done. I know that Mary and mother will come to me. Should I live to see them, God's name be praised.

THE DOCTOR'S POSTSCRIPT.

About the close of January, an elderly lady, and one much younger, came to the hospital. I felt at once that they had come for my patient. I said nothing, but pointed to his room. There was a scream, but not of pain. It was too full of gladness for that. My patient is growing stronger every day, and I suppose he will leave us by the middle of February.

I hold in my hands a noble gift the mother has bestowed upon the hospital. It is a check to cover the cost of a new window for the chapel of the hospital, to be an exact copy of the pictured window which had so much to do with her son's history that Christmas morning, and another check to reward most liberally the three young men who rang the bells at midnight—the bells that carried God's message to the poor soul so close to destruction.

GAINING BY LOSING.

GAINING BY LOSING.

I. CHRISTMAS IN PROSPERITY.

EDWARD WORTHINGTON, a weal-thy New York merchant, was on the high road to becoming a mil-lionaire. Every thing he touched seemed to turn to gold. His friends mar-velled at his daring ventures, but applauded the success that always came.

His home, in the most aristocratic quarter of the city, was as luxurious as could well be imagined, and was almost a treasure house of costly adornments and works of art. His family consisted of his wife and two daugh-ters. At the time this story opens, the latter had just graduated from a fashionable board-ing-school.

Their accomplishments were of the usual

order of girls brought up without any spe-
cial aim in life except to pursue the round
of fashionable amusements.

They were not at all to blame for this, for
their parents had never tried to inspire them
with any higher ambition than to carry themselves creditably in society as the daughters
of a successful merchant with the command
of almost unlimited wealth.

At school they had been courted and flattered by their companions, and every thing
had been made as easy as possible for them
by their teachers.

It would have been strange indeed if, under all the circumstances, they had developed
any thing but weak, selfish dispositions.

Their mother was a weak, selfish woman,
and their father's wisdom and energy found
their scope only in his business.

His home life included no care for his
family beyond surrounding them with what
wealth would buy, and what would fit them
for such society as that in which they moved.

It was a family without religious princi-

ples. It is true that now and then they at-
tended some church, but they had no interest
in practical religion, and were living only for
this world.

The winter of 18— found them in the
height of their prosperity preparing for a
grand party at their house on Christmas
Eve. They selected this time for the party
not from any interest they felt in Christmas
itself, but because it was a season of gayety
in their circle, and because they could then
secure the presence of a great throng.

They were determined to make it a great
affair, and if possible to eclipse all the sim-
ilar occasions in which they had taken part
in the earlier portion of the season.

Invitations were sent out to hundreds.
The decorators, the caterers, and others were
given *carte blanche*, and for some weeks there
was quite a hum of busy preparation for the
Worthington's Christmas party.

How shall I describe the magnificence of
that occasion? You can imagine the beautiful residence brilliantly lighted; the profu-

sion of rare flowers and plants in the halls
and stairways and wherever else they could
be put; the rooms crowded with guests, the
strains of music from the band, the dancing,
the supper, and the buzz of talk that went
on from the many who had accepted the
rich man's bidding to the feast.

As such gatherings go it was a great success. It was successful even when compared
with the many brilliant assemblies held in
such a city as New York.

Money makes many friends, and money
buys much splendor. Here there was no
lack of either, so that when the party was
over the Worthingtons had reason to con-
gratulate themselves upon having fairly out-
shone their neighbors, and were as happy as
people usually are under such circumstances.

The Christmas bells rang out their calls to
prayer and praise while the tired family
were sleeping off the effects of the previous
evening's fatigue and excitement.

No one in that home responded to the
call, and no one's heart there thrilled with

joy over the story of a Saviour's birth.
They would have resented the charge of
being heathen, but after all was it not a
heathenish life they lived?

What was it to them that One had been
born in a manger?

What was it to them that He had taught
men to be self-denying, and to trust not in
uncertain riches?

Although they lived in a Christian land,
there had not up to this time entered into
their lives any thing that distinguished them
from those who had never heard of Christ
and of His salvation.

The Christmas festival was to them only
a time of mirth and rejoicing, of exchang-
ing gifts, and of compliance with the world's
usages. It had no religious significance.

And so that Christmas time passed away.

II. CHRISTMAS IN ADVERSITY.

No one of the many guests who crowded
the house of Mr. Worthington on that Christmas Eve could have fancied so great a change
as that which took place in the fortunes of
the merchant before a year passed away.
His wealth seemed so secure, his sagacity
so great, that however probable it was that
other men might be submerged under the
wave of financial troubles, none thought that
he could be injured. And yet when the wave
passed it left Mr. Worthington a poor man.
His vast possessions were swept away, and
he was utterly ruined. It is hard to describe
just how the calamity fell upon him. It was
one of those sudden, unexpected events that
no one can accurately recount.

He had grown very bold in his ventures,
had put his whole estate into the risk, and
was amazed when the result was so different from what all the probabilities had indicated.

It was not an ordinary failure, but a thorough sweeping away of all that he had. His house and its contents, his securities, his business, every thing had to go. Ile had staked heavily, and if the result had been as he wished he would have been a millionaire, but it was just the opposite. He had not shown ordinary prudence. He made the one awful, fatal blunder and lost his all.

His obligations were so far beyond his resources that the latter seemed small indeed, and his creditors, alarmed lest his failure should lead to the failure of others, were clamorous for settlement, and would accept no compromise.

It might have been possible under some circumstances to have saved enough, by the favor of his creditors, to have enabled him to go on again, but his creditors happened to be men whose fears made them merciless, and they pressed him heavily.

It required days and weeks for the once prosperous merchant to realize the wonderful change that had come in his affairs, and it was only when the need of rousing him·

self to do something to gain bread for his
family was forced upon him that he saw
how great was the wreck of all his hopes
and plans.

It was just before Christmas when the unhappy family left the beautiful home where
but a year before they had made such a dis-
play of their wealth.

Now bowed down with sadness, they took
their way to an obscure street in the great
city to the few rooms they had rented, and
where they were to begin life under such
changed circumstances.

The little street seemed so dingy, and the
mean rooms were so mean, that their first
evening there was an evening spent mainly
in lamentations and tears.

When Christmas Eve came their minds
went back to the brilliant scene of the pre-
ceding year, and they uttered bitter com-
plaints that of all those who had on that
occasion assembled in their home not one
remembered them in their poverty. All had
forsaken them. They were as much alone as

if they had been strangers newly arrived in the great city.

It was a sad evening, and as the father looked around at his family he said—"Well, this is terrible. Here we are alone and poor, when only a year ago we had all that heart could wish. It is bad enough to be poor, but it seems worse to be as utterly forgotten as we seem to be. But there is one thing I have learned, and that is to put very little reliance in people who can be bought and sold for money. There must be some people in the world different from those we have had to do with. There surely must be some who are less selfish, and who will cling closer than the idle throng whom our money drew to our doors."

Just then there was a knock at the door, and there entered an old man, who announced himself as a neighbor living in the next house, He had a good-natured, cheery manner that quite won the hearts of the saddened family, and then any visitor was welcome on such a night.

The neighbor had come in, he said, seeing they were strangers, to invite them to the Christmas service in the little chapel down the street the following morning.

And he went on in his bright way to tell them about the affairs of the little chapel, and the good work the Lord was doing among the poor of that neighborhood.

They listened to him with more interest than they ever supposed they could have in such matters, and in response to his earnest invitation promised to be there on Christmas morning.

When he was gone Mrs. Worthington said, "Edward, this is about as strange as any thing else in our year's history—this going to a poor mission chapel on Christmas morning. Well, I'm glad you promised to go, for it is getting to be perfectly dreadful living here without knowing any one, and as we are deserted by the rich we may as well make some friends among the poor."

And so on the next morning they all went to the Christmas service in the chapel. It was a very humble building, and the congregation was made up of very humble people.

There were a few people present, men and women who preferred doing without the luxurious appointments of the grand churches in the city that they might add to the comfort and benefit of their less favored brethren.

The service was hearty and enthusiastic. The music had a gladsome ring to it, and the responses seemed to come from the heart. The sermon was very simple. The preacher told over again the old, old story, but told it with a freshness and vividness that made it seem all new.

All new it certainly was to the Worthingtons, and they listened with absorbing interest. No eloquent words they had before heard impressed them so deeply as this plain discourse which was so devoid of all attempts at ornament.

Perhaps their spirits were in just the mood to be touched.

But be that as it may, they left that chapel when the service was over with new feelings, and with the firm conviction that life must have in it a deeper meaning than they had yet found if the Son of God could humble Himself to live here among men.

There was not any sudden conversion. They did not become at once devout Christian people, but a change began to come over them. One good thought led on to another. One new friend brought another, and somewhat to their own surprise they found themselves part and parcel of the mission congregation and taking a deep interest in its affairs.

They gradually became more and more accustomed to their changed circumstances, and as new interests were formed, and as Mr. Worthington found employment where he could support his family in tolerable comfort, they began to be much more hopeful and happy.

The mother and daughters found their sympathies drawn out towards their poor neighbors, and ere long were led to assist in the school and in the different societies which existed in the mission for Christian work.

And so step by step, the Lord led these people, showing them how vain is man's trust in his riches, how fickle are the friends that come only in prosperity, and what undeveloped capacities there are which only the touch of affliction can draw out.

So they were led on and on, until as years passed by they became very earnest Christians, and were able to say, "It is good for us that we have been afflicted."

But it was a hard lesson. Their hold of the world had been very tenacious, their selfishness had been very great, and their forgetfulness of God had been extreme. Nothing but so heavy a blow could have saved them from going on in that way whose record is summed up in the significant expression, "Without God in the world."

Now all was changed, and they found themselves the possessors of peace of mind and genuine satisfaction which were not theirs in their days of wealth.

III. CHRISTMAS IN EARNEST.

Ten years have passed away since the old man who lived in the next house paid his friendly visit to the Worthingtons to invite them to the Christmas service.

The good old man knew not what happy results would follow his neighborly deed, and he has long since gone to his rest.

It is Christmas Eve again, but we do not find the Worthingtons living in the humble street near the chapel. No, they have removed to a better house, for Mr. Worthington is again a prosperous business man. He has won his way onward until now he is again a man of means. Not the wealthy man we first knew, for he has given up those reckless ventures which before resulted so disastrously, and is now content with more moderate returns.

He is steadily acquiring influence, and is making his power felt in the business world.

But the family have not returned to the old life they lived in their former prosperity.

They have no desire to take up the senseless round that once occupied them. They have but little desire to live in the glare and glitter which they once affected.

They can never think of their former condition without being glad that they are so happily out of it now.

Their new prosperity has not weakened their love for the little mission chapel where they first learned how real and how noble life has become since the Son of God has taught us its possibilities.

Many warm friendships were made there which have grown stronger with years, and many a tie binds them to the pastor and people of the mission.

This Christmas Eve, as has been his custom for a few years past, Edward Worthington calls together a different class of persons to partake of the good cheer of his home. Now it is not his rich neighbors, but the poor who come at his invitation, and many a needy child, many toil-worn men and women, have learned that there is always some-

thing for them in Edward Worthington's
home on Christmas Eve. The mission people feel at their ease with him, for they know
that his heart sympathizes with them. They
rejoice at his prosperity as they see the good
he is doing with his wealth, and no one of
them has a hard thought because he is rich
while they are poor. "Why," says one of
them, "a man like Worthington who has been
down nearly as poor as we are, and has got
his money honestly and uses so much of it
for others—why, he's the sort of man to have
it. 'The Lord bless him.'"

And so to-night these people find brightness and welcome and comfort in their friend's
house, and leave him with benedictions.

If again he should be prostrated by calamity, will he be without friends? Will he go
out from his home to bear his burden alone

Ten years ago he was living for the perish-
able things of this life, but now he and his
are trying to lay up treasures in heaven.

PANSY'S PREPARATIONS FOR CHRISTMAS

PANSY'S PREPARATIONS FOR CHRISTMAS.

A GRANDMOTHER'S STORY.

HE was "Heart's-Ease" to every one, and so we called her Pansy. She was a bright, cheery little creature, full of sunshine, and when she was taken away our home seemed very dark indeed. She was taken from us by the Good Shepherd only eight years from the day she came to us. Her coming filled many hearts with gladness, but her departing made many more sad.

"If only we could have kept her here," we used to say, but now that time has rolled on we have learned to say, "The Lord gave, and the Lord hath taken away, blessed be the name of the Lord."

We know that she is at rest in Paradise, and we hope to see her again where all is gladness, and where suffering can not come. It was very hard to give her up. She was such a gentle little thing, with so many winning ways, that she became the very joy of our lives, and we all thanked God in our prayers that she had come to be the brightener of our home.

It was very amusing to see the joy of her big brothers, —there were three of them, great tall fellows,—when the baby was born. Being the only girl in the family they regarded her at first with great wonderment, and finally yielded themselves absolutely to her sway. Never did fair lady have such loyal followers as did she.

These big brothers were attentive to her every command, and were ready to go through fire and water to serve her.

Many were the contests between them as to which of the three should do the most for her ladyship. It is true that sometimes their attentions were very clumsy and blundering, but she seemed to know their devotion, and rewarded them with her bright sunny smile, and they were happy. When she began to talk their delight was unbounded, and her first efforts at pronouncing their names seemed to them the most wonderful performance they had ever listened to.

She had many instructors in articulation, and it is to be feared she was often wearied with the zeal not only of her brothers but of all the household in teaching her to say the little words and phrases that sounded so quaint, but so pretty, as she uttered them.

The Christmas trees that were prepared for Pansy were wonderful things. These big brothers claimed the right to select the trees, and to decorate them. The decorations were not very rich, for we were not a wealthy family. We had enough, but not overmuch of this world's goods. We have never known poverty, and we have never known riches.

But if there was nothing very costly on Pansy's trees, there was certainly a great variety; jack-knives, and jig-saws, under the

boys' loving management produced marvels
in the shape of dolls, doll-houses, Noah's arks,
boats, and the like, and there were brilliant-
ly-colored pictures, the product of hours spent
in the old attic by James, the artist of the
family.

Well, these Christmas trees gave great delight to the little one, as certainly they did
to the older people. In very few homes
could the Saviour's birthday have been cele-
brated with more rejoicing, and so year by
year we welcomed its coming. Our little
daughter grew more and more attractive,
and she was surrounded with an atmosphere
of affection. And what was best of all she
seemed to return all our love, and paid us
back smile for smile. How greatly we loved
her, and how greatly we enjoyed her.

Sometimes we older people had our day
dreams, and we pictured to ourselves what
our little one would be when she grew up to
womanhood, but our brightest pictures for
her were not so bright as the future the dear
Lord had prepared for her.

We thought of a happy, useful, beautiful life here on the earth, but He intended a blissful existence in Paradise.

We know now that His ways are wiser than ours, and that it was in loving kindness to little Pansy that He called her from all the sorrows of this life, and carried her, in all her joyous innocence, into the life of perfect gladness. She never knew what sorrow really was. Her stay here was made bright and happy by the love that surrounded her, and long before she could realize that there were burdens to be borne, and temptations to be met, she was ushered into the abode of the blessed, where she is growing in all the sweetness of her spirit in the nearer presence of the Lord.

But I started out to tell you of her last Christmas with us, or rather of the last preparations she made for the blessed Christmas time. She was not content to be a receiver of the good gifts of others, but must, in her way be a giver too; so when she was a very little girl she began to add to the load that hung upon the Christmas tree. It was but little that she could do, but we all learned to prize her little gifts as among our choicest treasures.

Early in November, when the snows commenced to fall, we knew that the dear child had begun her preparations. During a part of each day we would miss her, and now and then there were packages of bright colored worsteds that she would commission me to buy. Of course I never knew what they were for, or if I ventured a guess I was hushed by a tiny finger on my lips, and a pleading voice that said—"It's a secret, mamma, and no one must know till Christmas time."

When that last December opened, it found our house in deep sadness. A sickness that we could not account for, had taken hold of our little one, and for some days the doctor's visits were looked forward to with great anxiety. But there were only a few days of sharp pain, and then in our blindness and affection we thought the danger all over.

It is true the little one had to stay in her bed, but we all thought she would be about again as merry as ever. Well, it did seem as if she must recover, and so we dismissed our anxieties, and hopefully waited, but it was ordered otherwise by the great loving Father. Pansy's sickness was one from which there was no recovery, and there she lay during those winter days growing weaker instead of stronger, and we all the time hoping that we could keep her with us. She was fading away from us even while we were looking for the change that would restore her.

I suppose now we might have seen how utterly hopeless was her condition if we had not longed so ardently for her recovery.

And she was so bright and cheerful too. There was but little pain, only that dreadful weakness that became more and more decided.

But during the few weeks she lay there as white as a lily, her little fingers were busy, and her brain was full of plans for keeping

Christmas. It was my privilege to be the dear child's confidant and assistant in her preparations for making others happy. She told me what she wanted to do for each one, and I was permitted to help her.

She did not know how many were the silent tears I shed over the little tasks she transferred to me, nor how during those last few days I struggled to control my almost breaking heart.

She lingered on until Christmas Day and then we all knew that the end had come. She knew it too. I have reason to believe since that she knew it long before we did, and with sweet patience was waiting the hour when she should be called to a better home.

It was just towards the dawn of the winter's day that we all came together in her room. Her bed was strewn with the many little things she had prepared for Christmas gifts. I had placed them where she could see them, at her request, and she wanted to give them " with her own hands,"

she said. She could not wait till morning,
she told us, and so we came to receive our
gifts. I need not tell you what they were.
They were only little things, such as a little child would select, and such as her own
hands would have finished if she had had
the strength. There were names worked in
worsted, purses, needle-books, such things
as these. No stranger would have valued
them, but to us they were treasures indeed.

I do not know how it was, but as we went
up to the bedside one by one to receive our
gifts we knelt down, and her dear hands having bestowed the gift were placed tenderly
on our heads, as if somehow her benediction
must go with the gift.

And I am sure it did, for through all these
long years when Christmas Day comes we
fancy we still feel the touch of those hands
as we felt it then when we knelt by Pansy's
bedside, and it has been to us a help through
life's trials, for it has reminded us of the welcome and the affection that await us in Par
adise.

She could not say much to us, but her
eyes were eloquent with happiness.

Well, the last gift was made, and the little
hands were uplifted from her father's head,
for it was her fancy to give his last of all,
when I saw the change coming. A shadow
passed over her face, there was a spasm of
pain, and then quietly she fell asleep and
awoke no more. Our "Heart's-Ease" was in
Paradise.

I will not tell you how much we missed
that blessed sunbeam from our home, nor
how lonely we all seemed without her.

Seeing you all so busy preparing for Christmas reminded me of my dear one's preparation for the last Christmas she spent with us.
We have her little gifts yet. My boys have
grown up to be men, but I know that they
keep as among their dearest possessions Pansy's gifts which they received as they knelt
at her bedside so many years ago that Christmas Day when He who was once a child
called our darling home, and folded her in
His loving arms. And I've told you the

story too that you may sometimes have the thought come to you that these little things you receive from each other, as this happy season comes, may have a value you can not see at once. They may be freighted with the love and devotion of some who before another Christmas comes will not be with us here.

HOW TO ILLUSTRATE THE STORIES.

HOW TO ILLUSTRATE THE STORIES.

HEN these stories are read aloud in families, or at Sunday-school festivals, at Christmas time, they can readily be illustrated by tableaux and carols.

The following directions will show how to do this, and the ingenuity of parents, teachers, and others will provide still further illustrations.

1st. There should be a reader who, having studied a story in advance, should on the occasion of the public reading stand near the platform where the illustrations are to be given.

2d. In almost every parlor with folding

doors the rear room could be used for the tableaux. In halls, etc., a platform with curtain could easily be constructed.

3d. The reader and the persons selected to give the illustrations should have one or two rehearsals in advance.

4th. At the time of the reading, when the reader reaches a part where a tableau is to be shown, let him pause in the story. Consider the tableau as a picture of the scene

5th. The music for the carols can usually be rendered by a concealed chorus of ten or twelve children. Any familiar carols can be used.

6th. The numbers in brackets in the stories refer to the tableaux, etc., described in the following pages.

ILLUSTRATIONS.

Uncle John's Christmas Party.

1. Uncle John enters, arranges his straps, brushes his hat, cleans his glasses, reads his paper, examines contents of his pockets.

2. Aunt Susan enters, walks arm in arm with Uncle John, point out to each other the sunset clouds, etc.

3. Enter the cook, drops the pan, storms over it, remembers herself, picks it up gently, etc.

4. Enter Dickey Diggs, absent-minded— pantomime at discretion.

5 Enter the twins, carrying something, one going fast, the other slowly. They begin to do some work in same way.

6. Here all enter,—servants, Uncle John, and Aunt Susan. Pantomime.

7. Motley collection of people present. Uncle John receiving the lawyer.

8. The doctor's entrance.

9. The group around the table. During

this part of the story Uncle John and the guests follow its course in pantomime.

The Tramps' Christmas Eve.

I.

The interior of the living room: an old man at the right of the fireplace, an old woman on the left, in old-fashioned chairs; a young woman by a table sewing.

Pantomime to follow as the story is read:

1.—Sadness of the three.

2.—Mary weeping.

3.—They turn toward each other as the farmer speaks.

4.—The knock at the door—change of position.

II.

Entrance of the three servants, Betty, Michael, and Jonas. Awkward bowing and scraping. Unfolding of the petition. Permission given. Joy of the servants. Exit.

III.

The interior of the old kitchen. The servants having a merry time.

Pantomime follows the course of the story. During the ghost story gestures of terror, etc. At the knocking at the door all start up, etc.

IV.

Enter the two tramps.

Follow in pantomime the course of the story.

V.

The entrance of Mr. and Mrs. Warren and Mary.

Group themselves to watch the dancing. Pantomime follows the course of the story.

VI.

Here all rise excitedly.

Mary rushes to him and falls down at his feet.

The Belated Christmas Guests.

1. Tableau. A group around a wood fire (a pile of wood with red paper to represent

the flames will do), torn pieces of white paper scattered around will represent the snow.

2. Entrance of the second party, wrapped
up with cloaks, etc., covered with snow, looking very tired.

3. All grouped together.   One man standing, book in hand.   At intervals all sing some
Christmas carols.

4. A shout outside, all startled, rise to
their feet.   Enter Farmer Larch.

Robert Rounce.

1. Enter Robert Rounce as described.
2. Enter Dick Lay.
3. Group of merry children.
4. Bob and the children on their way to
the woods.
5. Their return with the evergreens.
6 Carol singing.
7. Children separate.
8. Soft music.
9. Children rush out to meet him.
10. Bob on his way home

11. At work. Carpenters, etc.

12. More workmen come on.

13. Singing.

14. Chorus.

The Crew of the Sea Gull.

1. Imitations outside of the whistling and moaning of the storm.

2. The crew huddled together. The sand-bank may be represented by canvas cast over chairs, etc. Turn the lights down. Scatter pieces of white paper to represent snow.

3. A chorus outside singing a carol. The crew join in with them.

4. The two parties rush back and forth across the stage.

5. Enter the old clergyman.

6. Here sing a number of carols. Singers concealed, or else represent the interior of a chapel.

Aunt Kitty's Christmas Tree.

1. Tableau. Interior of a room. Old woman in chair sewing. Two cats on rug before her.

2. The same. A few boys and girls very plainly dressed peeping around the room— then standing before her as if questioning her.

3. Interior of a shop. Quaint old man behind counter. Aunt Kitty buying toys. Clarence watching.

4. Interior of room again. Three boys as if questioning her.

5. The three boys trimming the Christmas tree—then hiding themselves out of sight in closet.

6. Aunt Kitty and the dozen or so of children looking in amazement at the Christmas tree.

7. Clarence rolling out on the floor. The surprise of all.

8. The room filled with people, each having something for Aunt Kitty. Aunt Kitty's entrance with the poor children.

Reuben Reubenson.

1. Tableau. A gray-haired man, in an arm-chair before an open fire. A frame-work of canvas or paper painted may be used to represent an old-fashioned fireplace. Costume, any old-fashioned suit. Attitude, intent watching the fire.

2. Burst of music outside. Concealed chorus behind curtains, or in another room. One verse sung merrily. Then pause as reader goes on. Old man imitates the movements described by the reader, first looking into the chimney, then going to window.

3. Here may be sung any familiar carols. Two verses of, say, two carols, in rapid succession

4. A couple more carols in same way.

5. Music sung more and more faintly, as if the singers were passing down the street.

6. Sing very gently, simply hum the tune.

7. Old man asleep in chair. Santa Claus comes down chimney, walks about, then passes out.

8. A curtain concealing Christmas tree is

withdrawn. This tableau, in small room, could be omitted.

9. One or two verses of the old hymn "Adeste fideles," sung slowly ·by concealed chorus. At end of this the old man need not appear again. Draw curtains. Or imitate the actions described by the reader and have the old man pass out when the reader describes his going to church.

10. Imitate the tolling of a church bell, either upon piano, or by means of a bell outside.

The Christmas Chimes.

Imitations of ringing the changes on the bells, and carols can be played on the piano during the reading of the first chapter, and at the end of the whole story.

Gaining by Losing.

The contrast between the condition of the family in affluence and in poverty may be illustrated.

www.ingramcontent.com/pod-product-compliance
Lightning Source LLC
Chambersburg PA
CBHW020609030726
47497CB00007B/2148